The Ghost at the Window

by Elyssa Warkentin

Paperback ISBN 978-1-78705-755-5
ePub ISBN 978-1-78705-756-2
PDF ISBN 978-1-78705-757-9

Published by Orange Pip Books
335 Princess Park Manor, Royal Drive, London, N11 3G
www.orangepipbooks.com

Cover design by Brian Belanger

Chapter One

Janey Wiggins raced through the dark London streets. The trickle of light let off by the thin crescent moon was veiled by clouds, and in the absence of lamplight she could barely see a foot in front of her face. The lamplighters had not yet made their way through the maze of East London streets, but Janey had lived in the neighbourhood for all of her eleven years, and she knew it like the back of her hand.

Janey was a tall girl for her age, with plain brown hair tied back with a simple ribbon. She was growing so fast that her dresses were always a little bit short, worn at the elbows, and fraying where her mother had taken down the hems. She had quick brown eyes that flashed speedily between mischievous smiles and fits of temper.

Panting now, she flew across the cobbles. Her feet pounded and her legs pumped hard, muscles burning with the strain. Quickly, she dodged through an archway that stretched between two dingy buildings and plunged into the inky blackness beyond. She crouched down behind a row of rubbish bins, wrinkling her nose. The stench was overpowering: rotting vegetable scraps and worse, the leavings of the businesses that inhabited the surrounding buildings that were too rotten to even appeal to the starving animals that frequented the alleys. But it was her best bet for safety. She withdrew further into the darkness, pressing into the bin beside her to make herself as small and invisible as possible as she tried to catch her breath.

For a moment there was silence. Janey heaved a sigh of relief. That had been a close call – she'd been out playing in the streets with her friend Rose, like they did every evening, but this time she'd allowed herself to be distracted by the grumblings of her empty belly, and then had been lost in daydreams of extravagant meals. She was a daydreamer by habit, but this time it had been dangerous. They'd almost been caught by the Vigilance Committee thugs who patrolled the streets after sundown each night, acting like they ruled them, like they could decide who had the right to use them, and when. Rose had dashed off down the street at the sight of the group of swaggering men, and Janey sprinted away in the opposite direction, hoping the gang would give up on the idea of pursuit. She knew they considered street girls like her to be a menace – a danger to the respectable folk who lived in the area. Somehow, *respectable* always seemed to mean *rich* to people like this. Janey wasn't sure what they'd do with her if they caught her, but she knew it wouldn't be pleasant. They'd treat her like a criminal, probably, just for being out on the street after dark. A pickpocket, or something worse. Her face burned at the thought.

She sagged against the bin. She was still hungry. She'd had her milk and bread with her mother when they'd risen that morning, and a cup of weak tea, too, but there was nothing else in their cupboard. Her mother had hugged her apologetically and taken up her basket to walk the three miles to Covent Garden to sell flowers with the other vendor women.

"When I return, I'll stop at the corner stall and we'll

have a meat pie each," she had promised Janey, kissing her cheek.

Janey had kissed her back and smiled. "Good luck, then, mother."

But at that, her mother had only sighed.

"It's not luck that earns our bread, Janey – it's hard work. That's something you'd do well to remember." She was always pestering her to take up odd jobs and earn some money.

Now, in the still darkness, Janey's stomach growled again at the memory of her mother's promise.

"Soon," she told herself. "It's almost dinner time. Just a little longer."

Suddenly, she sat up straighter. Her keen ears picked up the sound of boots on cobbles. Were they coming nearer?

She strained to hear. The footsteps had slowed, but they were definitely coming closer.

Closer.

Closer still.

Janey held her breath. She saw a figure outlined against the entrance to the alley. It paused for a moment, and soon it was joined by several others.

"Did you see which way she went?" a voice asked lowly.

Her blood froze in her veins. She knew that voice. It was Mr. Crawford, the chairman of the Vigilance Committee and the cruelest of the gang.

"Nah, I think we lost her," another answered. Mr. Crawford cursed under his breath.

"Let's hope the little street rat makes for the sewers – where she belongs."

The men surrounding Mr. Crawford laughed. It almost seemed to Janey that they were looking straight at her even if she knew it was too dark in the alley for her to be seen. After a moment they moved on, hurrying away down the side street.

Janey waited a minute then burst out from her hiding spot in a sudden explosion of speed. Without a backwards glance, she raced out of the alley, turning in the opposite direction, making for the busier Commercial Street just a hundred yards away. She was close – so close to the street that she could hear snippets of conversation as people passed up and down, could hear the clip-clop of horse hooves as cabbies carried wealthier Londoners through her poor neighbourhood and home to their comfortable beds and well-stocked pantries.

The single room in which she lived with her mother was on the other side of this street, just over the baker's shop that stood at the corner of Commercial Street and New Road. If she could make it to the side entrance of her building, she would be safe, and her mother would come home. They would eat and talk about their days and maybe – if Janey were very lucky – her mother would have brought home a newspaper that they would read together by the flame of a single candle, huddled in the small bed they shared. Janey loved to read, but it was rare that they could afford even the small expense of a newspaper.

Her heart pounded. She was so close to home that she could almost smell it - the delicious baking bread that wafted up into her room every morning, the laundry that hung drying in the winter sun. Ahead of her, the warm streetlights on Commercial Street had been lit, and the light spilled out, calling to her. She was almost there.

And then, with a sharp cry of victory that seemed to come out of thin air, a hand shot out of the dark and latched onto Janey's arm, stopping her dead in her tracks.

Chapter Two

Janey gasped in pain as the hand around her forearm tightened, holding her fast.

"Got you!" a voice hissed in her ear.

Janey twisted around. Her stomach fluttered in dismay. It was just her luck, she thought – she'd been captured by Jim Crawford, the son of the leader of the Vigilance Committee, and one of the roughest boys she knew. He was big for his age – tall and muscular – and his mouth was twisted in an ugly sneer. There was no way she could get away.

"Janey Wiggins!" he said. He sounded surprised. "I ain't seen you since you left school."

Janey groaned. She'd attended the free Charity School in Hunton Road with all of the neighbourhood children, including Jim Crawford and the rest of his gang of bullies, though he'd been a year ahead of her. She'd learned to keep her head down, to stay out of their way and make the best of her lessons. But when she'd turned 10 years old, her mother had sat her down and carefully explained that there was no need for a poor flower-peddler's daughter to have any more of an education than she had already had; that it was a waste of time when she could be helping out and earning money. Janey hadn't been to school since.

"What're you doing, wandering about the streets like a common thief, *girl*?" He spat out the last word like an insult.

Janey flushed. "What are *you* doing, Jim Crawford?

Wandering the streets like a common thug?"

She tried to tug away from his grip, but the more she pulled, the harder he dug his fingers into her arm. There would be bruises tomorrow, she thought.

Suddenly, she felt very alone. No one in the world knew where she was. There was no one to help her. Janey shivered in her thin, cotton dress. The colourful shawl her mother had knit for her the winter before was a help in weather like this, but she'd been outside all day and was chilled nearly to the bone.

Jim shook her. "Wait till my father sees what I've caught. A month in the Reformatory will teach you your place."

Janey shuddered. The Juvenile Reformatory was little better than a prison for children. "You can't send me to the Reformatory! I've done nothing wrong."

Jim scoffed.

"Wandering the streets alone after dark? If you're not a criminal now, you will be one soon. Who're they going to believe? Me? Or street trash like you?" He shook her arm again.

"Let go of me!" Suddenly, Janey was more furious than scared. She was cold and hungry and miserable, and all she wanted to do was go home to her mother and her dinner. Jim had no right to detain her! She felt anger bubbling up inside her.

"Respectable girls know their place is at home," he

said. He pulled her close and spoke into her ear, his voice low and dangerous. "You've got no business being out. You're trouble – you always were. Brown-nosing at school; pretending to be so clever, so good. But I know you, Janey Wiggins. Your mother's a filthy beggar and you don't even *have* a father. You're nothing."

"My mother," she replied furiously, "is not a beggar. She's an honest woman. More honest than you!" She'd been angry before, but at this new insult made her shake with rage.

Just then, Janey saw a flicker of movement in the shadows behind Jim. A small face peeped out from the recessed doorway of a closed shop. It was Rose! Janey had thought she'd be half-way to her home by now. She should have known the loyal girl would never abandon her.

Rose was tiny - six years old and small for her age, but she was brave. Janey had never known her to back down from a fight. If they were going to make a move, they'd have to do it now, before Jim summoned his father and the rest of the Vigilance Committee men. There'd be no escape for her then.

She braced herself, widening her stance on the uneven cobbles, and then gave a low whistle that she and Rose used as a private signal between them when they were playing with other girls. Jim started back and looked at her in confusion, but by then Rose was darting out of the shadows with a holler, stomping on his feet and crashing into his body with all her weight.

He staggered, unprepared for the attack, and his grip on Janey's arm loosened. Quick as lightning, Janey slipped from his grasp and propelled herself down the street, Rose once again at her side.

The street behind them rang with Jim's curses.

"We'll pay for that if he ever catches us again," Rose panted.

"Well, we won't let that happen, will we?" Janey said.

She reached out and grabbed Rose's hand, tugging her around corners and darting between buildings, putting as much distance as she could between them and Jim Crawford. Rose wasn't as fast as Janey – few of their neighbourhood playmates were – but she was small and smart. She could squeeze into spaces Janey would never think to attempt, and was light enough to clamber up drainpipes that would collapse under the older girl's weight. It would be safer still for them to separate, to let Rose make her own way, but Janey found she was strangely unwilling to let go of the girl's hand.

When at last they slowed their pace, they were more than a mile away and there'd been no footsteps behind them for many minutes.

"How did you find me?" Janey asked. She was annoyed with herself for getting caught, but more annoyed with Rose for putting herself in danger. "You were supposed to go straight home!"

The girl shrugged. "I wasn't going to leave you out alone with those thugs on your tail, was I? I had to make sure you were alright."

Janey frowned. "I can take care of myself, Rose."

"Oh, Janey," Rose sighed. "I knew you'd make for that alley. You *always* hide there. I've seen you! So, I pretended to go one way to get rid of Crawford and his men, but then I doubled back to check on you."

"Clever girl!" Janey praised. She continued, a bit quieter, "Thank you, Rose. You really saved me, there."

And truly, she was impressed. It had been an excellent ploy: she'd have to remember it, she thought to herself. You could never tell when these things might come in handy.

Rose blushed and ducked her head, tugging on her blonde plait. "It's no more than you'd do for me."

Janey's heart warmed. "Come on," she said, taking Rose's hand again. "Let's get you home."

Chapter Three

There were no more run-ins with the Vigilance gang, but Janey and Rose kept their eyes open nonetheless. Janey didn't want her carelessness to endanger them once again. They kept to the main streets - the well-lit thoroughfares full of people, knowing that there was safety in the company of strangers. No matter how prejudiced the men were against street girls, they were careful to always appear kind and fair in public.

Rose lived off Hunton Road, very close to the Charity School. Even now, Janey's heart clenched each time she passed the school. As much as she could, she avoided Hunton Road for that reason. It was a reminder to her not to hope for anything better. She tucked her head down as she and Rose passed by, trying not to think about the time she had spent within those brick walls.

"School is not for the likes of us, my girl," her mother had said when Janey turned ten and the time had come for her to leave it behind for good. "You might as well get that through your head early rather than late."

Janey shook her head to dislodge the memory. She was used to ignoring her disappointments by now. It almost always worked.

They rounded the corner of Duval Road and came to the steps that led up to Rose's home. Rose pushed open the door with a clatter, and winced at the noise.

"Janey," Rose said nervously, "You'd better not come

in with me. If Henry's here, he'll be angry."

Henry was Rose's older brother, and he was the only family Rose had left. Her mother, like far too many other people who lived in the East End, was ill with the fevers and terrible coughing fits of tuberculosis - an illness that was dreaded because it killed so many people, and those who survived took so long to recover. TB, as it was called, spread quickly and easily from person to person. Doctors had decided that those infected must be isolated in hospitals until they were well again. Rose's mother had been away at the hospital for many weeks now, so ill that Rose had not been allowed into the hospital to visit her. The doctors said she was lucky – she would recover – but it would take time. In the meantime, Rose and Henry were on their own, doing their best to keep the household running. Henry was sixteen – old enough to work as a dock hand at the London docks, where days were long and hard. He brought home food for Rose when he remembered, but she often went hungry. Janey knew the girl missed her mother fiercely.

"Why should he be angry?" Janey asked. She visited Rose in her rooms often, just as Rose visited her in hers. They were almost like sisters, they were so close.

Rose's nervousness increased. "He's tired after work, and he needs to sleep. He doesn't like noise or light or anything to disturb him."

"Are you to sit in the dark, then?" Janey asked indignantly.

"Please," Rose said. "It's alright, Janey. He's just so

tired."

Janey sighed. The thought of little Rose – her little fairy, she sometimes called her – sitting hungry in the dark while her brother slept filled Janey with sadness. She kicked at the door in frustration.

Above them, a window screeched as it was pulled roughly open. A head poked out, quickly followed by a shaking fist.

"Rose!" Henry bellowed – for it was he, woken from his night's sleep. "Stop standing around, gossiping in the street like an old woman. Get inside! I ought to send you out to the soap factory to earn your keep like the rest of us. Stop chattering and get inside so a fellow can sleep in peace!"

Janey was horrified.

"He wouldn't really, would he?" she whispered. The soap factories paid next to nothing for extremely taxing work. Little Rose would never last!

"Don't worry," Rose said. She'd gone a bit pale, but she put on a plucky face. "His bark is worse than his bite." She kissed Janey's cheek and darted through the door.

Janey stood on the street for a moment. She heard Henry's voice rise in anger and then fall again into silence. When everything seemed calm, she turned away at last. She squeezed her fists tight and gritted her teeth. To think of Henry treating little Rose like that!

"Mercurial," her mother often called her. When Janey asked what the word meant, she explained that it was "changeable" and "unpredictable." Janey had looked it up in the big dictionary on the headmaster's desk at her school later that day, and seen that it could also mean "someone who is clever, lively, and quick." She felt proud when she read that. It described her well, she thought. Well, she *hoped*. But more often, she thought, it was just a nicer way of saying she had a terrible temper.

Suddenly, she couldn't hold in her anger any longer. Her rage at Jim Crawford's cruel taunts, at the Vigilance Committee's unfair treatment of her and her friends, at Henry's unkindness to little Rose, at her utter powerlessness to be where she wanted to be – at school. It felt like a fire was burning up in her belly, creeping outward into all her limbs, consuming every part of her. As if she would burst into flame if she didn't move.

And so, she ran.

She ran and ran, aimlessly down busy streets and dark alleys, not caring where her feet took her. She only wanted to feel the wind in her face and for a few minutes, at least – to be free. Chest heaving, Janey wove in and out of the labyrinth of East London's streets.

She knew these streets so well – she'd been playing on them since she'd been able to walk. There was a turn off, a narrow one, coming up on her left. Selby Passage ran between two tumble-down brick buildings on Pearl Street that were each hundreds of years old. One was boarded up and abandoned; the other was a little-used machinist's shop that had fallen into disrepair. She could cut through the passage, loop back around to Commercial Street, and be home to meet her mother when she returned from Covent Garden.

And then she saw it, looming ahead and just to her left. The buildings crowded close together, their shadows appearing as a deeper darkness that swallowed her up as she ran. She picked up speed, sprinting with a last burst of sizzling energy.

In the darkness of the passage, before she could turn or even react, she felt herself crash into a figure standing in the middle of the path. It was someone who was very tall and very sturdy; Janey felt as if she had run up against a brick wall.

She heard his startled exclamation as she fell back, staggering and toppling over in her shock. Her head bounced back onto the pavement, and the pain brought stars to her eyes. Then the stars began to swirl. They flashed blindingly, then faded to black, and she knew no more.

Chapter Four

Janey came to herself. Hours or mere minutes could have passed. A searing pain in the back of her head made it difficult to think, let alone open her eyes. The air was cool on her face, though, and judging by the sounds and smells around her, she thought she must still be lying at the entrance to Selby Passage. Not much time could have passed then, she thought with relief.

And then she heard the voices.

"Is she alright?" a man asked. He sounded annoyed.

"Just a nasty crack to the head, I think," another replied. "She should be right as rain once she regains consciousness."

Cautiously, she cracked open an eye. Her vision swam blurrily for a moment before she was able to focus, but she made out the warm glow of a lighted match being held over her. In the small circle of light that it cast, two worried faces looked down at her.

"Ah, there she is," the second voice murmured, sounding relieved. "Let's sit you up."

Janey felt careful hands cradling her head, lifting her up off the ground and propping her up against the wall of the brick building behind her.

Her head spun a little, and she reached up to clutch it in her hands.

"Does it pain you?" the man asked in a kindly sort of way. The match had gone out and Janey could no longer see anything more than the men's slight silhouettes.

"Of course it pains me," she snapped. Her mother had warned her of the dangers of talking to strange men on the street, but she was too angry now to be cautious. "What were you thinking, standing in the middle of the passage and blocking the way?" She struggled to remember what she could about what the men had looked like.

They were gentlemen – that much she knew. They weren't Crawford's men, and they weren't from her neighbourhood, either. Not with their top hats and thick wool coats and shiny leather shoes. No one in the neighbourhood dressed in such expensive garments. She'd rarely seen better.

The kindly man tutted. Instead of answering her question, he turned again to his companion. "We need some light. Do you have your pocket-lantern with you?"

The other man hissed in displeasure. "We can't risk being seen."

"We can't risk injuring a child, either," the kindly man replied pointedly. "Light the lantern. I need to examine her." The other sighed, but pulled a small lantern from his pocket and lit it, and Janey could see the men clearly for the first time.

The first man who'd spoken, the one who'd seemed annoyed with her for running into him, was tall and thin, with a long, pointed face and a prominent nose. His eyes had sparkled keenly in the light of the match. His friend, the man who had helped Janey sit up, had had a kindly face. He had been gentle and careful with her sore head.

"*Examine* me?" Janey asked, not understanding. "No! You'll not touch me!" She shrank back against the wall and gathered herself, preparing to run.

"My dear girl! Don't be afraid. I am a doctor. John Watson, at your service." He held out his hand.

Janey looked at him suspiciously. All she saw in his eyes was concern. Despite herself, she was tempted to trust him – just a little.

"Janey Wiggins," Janey replied, and hesitantly shook his hand.

Dr. Watson's companion was watching her closely. He did not look as kindly, but his eyes shone with a blazing intensity unlike anything Janey had seen before. She looked away, pretending not to have noticed.

"May I please examine you?" Dr. Watson asked. "I'd like to make sure you aren't injured before we send you on your way."

Janey nodded wordlessly. She'd never met a doctor before, but this one seemed very keen to help her. She wasn't used to anyone paying much attention to her at all.

"Thank you," he said kindly. "This shouldn't hurt much. I'm just going to check your skull – the bones in your head - to make sure you haven't broken anything." Carefully, he took her head in his hands and felt his way over her scalp. She winced in pain when he got to the back of her head.

"I'm sorry," he said sympathetically. "You've got a bit

of a lump, but nothing broken. It will be sore for a few days, but you'll recover quickly."

Janey nodded again. She'd hurt herself far worse in the past. Once, she'd even fallen off a cottage roof during a particularly thrilling game of hide-and-go-seek. She'd never needed a doctor before. Even if she had, she doubted her mother could afford to pay the fees. A thought struck her. Would they be expecting money in exchange for examining her?

"I can't pay you!" she said suspiciously. "I don't have any money."

"Heavens, no!" Dr. Watson cried, and he sounded almost hurt. "I wouldn't dream of it! Indeed, we must apologize to you. It was our carelessness in blocking this passage that caused your injury, after all."

With that, Janey remembered to be angry. After all, it was their fault that she had fallen. It was their fault that her head was aching so!

These streets were *hers*, hers and her friends'. Dr. Watson and his friend clearly did not belong.

"What are you even doing here?" she asked. "There's nothing in this passage for people like *you*."

"Nothing that need concern you," Dr. Watson's friend retorted coldly.

Dr. Watson sighed. "We are unfamiliar with this neighbourhood, and simply got lost looking for a friend's address," he said, looking pointedly at the other man, who rolled his eyes and turned away.

"Oh yes?" Janey said. She knew the man, kind as he was, must be lying. There could be no address on this bleak street that would interest a pair of such fine gentlemen. She decided to test them. "What was the address? I know every street and every building for miles around."

Dr. Watson looked uncomfortable. He cleared his throat, and turned to his friend.

The other man laughed shortly. "We don't need the help of a little street girl who can't even stand on her own two feet without falling over, but thank you very much."

At that, Janey saw red. She pulled herself up shakily against the brick wall. The world spun around her for a moment, but soon righted itself again.

"You're lying," she said loudly. "I don't know what you're doing here, but you're certainly not looking for a friend."

Dr. Watson made a sound of distress. "Please, child. Be calm. You must sit and recover a while longer."

His friend, Janey noticed, was looking at her sharply with eyebrows raised. Something she'd said had surprised him.

"I'm fine!" she said defiantly.

She turned toward Pearl Street and began to walk. She was so angry that tears stood in her eyes. It wasn't her fault that she was a street girl – and it was most unkind of this man to mock her for it. She would give anything to change her life, if only she had the chance. And anyway, she knew much more about these streets than either of these fine gentlemen. If they wanted to stand in the cold, dark alley all night, she would be happy to leave them to it. *I hope they freeze*, Janey thought crossly.

She was ten yards away when she finally noticed what she would have heard far earlier, if she hadn't been so upset - scuffling feet coming up Pearl Street at a breakneck speed.

"There she is!" a boy's voice shouted. "I see her, dad!"

Janey's eyes widened. The Vigilance gang was back, and Jim Crawford sounded angry. Without another thought she took to her heels, sprinting towards the safety of Commercial Street, cursing Dr. Watson and his strange friend as each step jolted her aching head. She didn't stop running until home was in sight.

Chapter Five

Janey looped around to the back of the bakers' shop on Commercial Street. A flight of rickety, rotting stairs led up to the lodgers' corridor that was lined with a dozen doors to a dozen tiny, cheap bedsits. The room she shared with her mother was tucked away under the back eaves of the building.

Looking up, a candle glowed in the window. It warmed Janey's heart to see it. Her mother was home, waiting for her with a warm pie and a warmer hug. Suddenly, Janey couldn't wait to see her mother and dashed up the stairs, taking them two at a time, bursting through the flimsy door.

Her mother looked up from where she sat in their only threadbare chair by the fire. She did not look pleased.

"Janey!" she scolded. "It's well past midnight. You know the rules, child!"

Suddenly Janey realized how late it was. She honestly hadn't heard the clocks chime in all the excitement of the evening. She hung her head.

"I'm sorry, mother."

Her mother sighed and beckoned her over, pulling her into a tight hug. "I worry about you, that's all."

"I know. I'm sorry," Janey said again, hugging her back.

Janey settled at her mother's feet, soaking up as much of the heat from the fire as she possibly could. She hadn't yet removed her shawl. The little fire was no match for the January temperatures, and their room was still cold.

She leaned against her mother's warm legs.

"Here." Her mother unwrapped her clean handkerchief and passed her a pie. Janey took it gratefully. The pastry was warm and she could smell the delicious meat and gravy within. She felt like she'd been running all day, she was ravenous.

"Good day?" Janey asked as they finished off the pies, licking their fingers clean of every last crumb.

Her mother shrugged. "Good enough. There's food, isn't there?"

Janey nodded. "Anything interesting happen?"

"Same old, same old. And what about you, love?"

Janey bit her lip. She didn't know how much she wanted to tell her mother about the adventures of the evening. She didn't want to worry her – she had worries enough of her own, but nor did she want to keep anything from her.

Her mother rapped her on the head with her knuckles – not hard enough to hurt, but not gently, either. "Well?"

"I ran into Jim Crawford. A boy from school."

"Crawford? Is he Ned's son? The Vigilance Committee man?"

Janey nodded and her mother winced in sympathy. The Vigilance gang was no kinder to women street-sellers than it was to girls.

"Any trouble?"

Janey shrugged. "A little. Nothing I couldn't handle. Rose helped, too."

Her mother looked suddenly furious. She jumped up and went to the window. Janey saw that her hands were clutched into fists.

"It's not right for grown men to bully little girls!" she burst out at last, so angry that her voice shook. Janey was used to her mother's fits of temper – their characters were astonishingly similar in that regard. She was only sorry she had vexed her.

"It's not right for them to bully *anyone*," Janey said. "Why do they do it, mother? What's it to them, what we do?"

Her mother sighed and turned from the window, dropping down to the floor to sit beside Janey.

"Don't waste your time trying to understand people like that," she said bitterly. "It's not worth the effort." Janey lay her head down in her mother's lap and closed her eyes while her mother stroked her hair, combing it out with her careful fingers.

She continued, "People are cruel, Janey. Their hearts are black with hatred. Men are cruel to women, the rich are cruel to the poor, and the strong are cruel to the weak. Those with power use it to hurt those without. It's always been this way, and it always will be."

Janey furrowed her brow in frustration. She wanted to understand, not just accept. *Why* should it always be this way?

Surely it wasn't right! How could her mother be so complacent about it?

"You should come with me tomorrow," her mother said. "With both of us selling, we'll make double the money."

Janey rolled her eyes. Her mother knew how much she hated selling flowers, but she was relentless in her campaign to hook Janey into the business.

"Fine. But see that you manage to earn something tomorrow, will you? Run some errands for Mrs. Hogarth or watch Mrs. Eastley's baby for a few hours? We really do need the money, Janey. I do wish you'd take up sewing and do some piece work again. I don't know what will become of you, I really don't!"

Janey nodded absently. At the mention of work, her mind had drifted away. While her mother talked about the potential jobs she might do, she got up and fetched her two most prized possessions from where they lay by the bed they shared - an old, faded copy of *Ernest Keen: Boy Detective*, and the rag doll her mother had sewn for her many years before. The book was the only one she owned, and she was lucky to have even that. Her mother had scrimped and saved for many months in order to purchase it for Janey's tenth birthday present. It had been the perfect gift. Janey loved to read, and worked hard at school, learning far quicker than most of her classmates. She'd read *Ernest Keen* hundreds of times by now, and never grew tired of it. She loved adventure stories more than anything. She sat back down beside her mother, snuggling her doll to her chest and opening the book in her lap.

Her mother kissed her head. "You're too old to play with dolls," she said, but her voice was full of fondness.

Janey gasped with mock anger. "Don't let Erna hear you say that!"

"Erna, is she? I thought you'd named her Annie?"

"Erna Keen. I renamed her after my book."

Her mother smiled and nodded.

"Well. We can talk about work later. Read me a chapter, will you?"

This was their much-loved evening pastime. Janey flipped through the pages to her favourite chapter and began to read.

Chapter Six

As pleasant as her evening with her mother had been, Janey was sad when she woke the next day, the cloud of gloom following her through her morning.

She did not, after all, run any errands for Mrs. Hogarth, nor did she watch Mrs. Eastley's baby. Instead, she buried her head in her pillow and tried to go back to sleep. At least in her dreams she was free to spend her time as she wished. Her mother had asked her to earn some money, but she felt bored almost to tears at the thought of any of the odd jobs she could do. Sewing? She shuddered. She'd rather walk Covent Garden with her mother, selling flowers – and she had no desire to do that, either.

She tossed and turned for almost an hour, but couldn't get back to sleep. Rose would be in school by now, she thought, if that oaf of a brother of hers allowed her to go. They'd be starting their lessons right about now. The sour taste of jealousy filled her mouth.

At last, Janey gave up on trying to sleep. There was no point worrying herself about things she couldn't fix. If she didn't want to sell flowers or run odd jobs, and she couldn't be in school, she was going to have to come up with a plan.

The only problem was she had no idea where to start.

Janey sat staring blankly at the wall for a while, but soon the silence settled heavily around her and her body twitched with the desire to move. She stood up, but there was barely room to pace in the little room. It was all very well, she thought crossly, for the Crawfords to tell women to stay at home when they had a mansion to live in and men working to support them! But her mother had to work. And Janey, herself, would go mad trapped in this tiny room all day and night. She could not do it!

Minutes later, Janey came barrelling out onto the street and plunged into the Commercial Street crowds. She didn't know where she was going, but knew she had to feel the wind on her face, again.

She walked as quickly as possible, enjoying the fresh winter air and the sun, not caring where she was headed. She couldn't wait until Rose's school day was finished and they could play together once again.

The Vigilance gang would be out again come sundown, surely, but for the time being, Janey was safe to enjoy the freedom of the streets.

After a time, Janey realized that she was unconsciously retracing the steps she had taken the night before. She was almost at Pearl Street, where Crawford and his men had surprised her, and also where she had crashed so disastrously into the strange men in Selby Passage.

She remembered how strange it was that such gentlemen should be standing in a dark passage. Suddenly curious, she decided to return to the passage to see if she could discover anything that might reveal what business they'd had there.

She quickly turned up Pearl Street, ducking into Selby

Passage a minute later. To her astonishment, she was not alone. Her two gentlemen were there again, leaning against the brick wall, gaping at her in surprise.

"Well, well!" exclaimed the man who had called himself Dr. Watson.

"Good morning, sir," she replied hesitantly.

"How lucky for us to run into you! We've been rather worried about you, young lady," Dr. Watson said. He was speaking rather quietly, Janey thought. "How is your head today?"

"It's fine, sir, thank you. A bit sore at the back, but better than it was."

Dr. Watson nodded. "Excellent. But why did you run off so quickly? Who on earth was chasing you?"

Janey explained about the Vigilance Committee, and how it waged a war on the East London streets; a war against poor people and street people and criminals and women.

"Idiots," Dr. Watson's friend muttered under his breath.

Janey face split into a surprised grin. "Indeed, sir."

"How on earth did you get away from them?" Dr. Watson asked.

"I'm very quick, sir," Janey said rather proudly. "I doubt there's a grown man in London who could best me at a race. My friends and I – we stick together and keep each other safe."

Dr. Watson nodded. Jane thought she might have seen a gleam of admiration in his eye.

Suddenly, with a flourish, Dr. Watson's friend sprang to life, offering his hand to Janey with a piercing glance and a cold, thin smile.

"Janey Wiggins," he said as he shook her hand, "My name is Sherlock Holmes. I am a detective, and I have a proposition for you."

"A detective?" Janey gasped. "A real-life detective? Like *Ernest Keen*?"

Mr. Holmes threw back his head and laughed. Even Dr. Watson smiled a little.

Janey's face flamed. If there was one thing she hated more than anything else, it was being laughed at. Why had she said something so stupid? She felt her temper rising and turned to stomp away, but Mr. Holmes's voice called her back.

"No, no. I'm sorry, Miss Wiggins. Forgive my rudeness. Please come back."

Chapter Seven

Janey stopped in her tracks. Mr. Holmes was no longer laughing.

She turned slowly back to the men who were still pressed against the passage's wall.

"Come back, please," Mr. Holmes requested. "I'm sorry I laughed! You simply surprised me with your reference. But we must keep our voices low and stay out of sight of the street as much as possible. Please, Miss Wiggins, come back into the passage. We must be discrete."

Janey's curiosity overcame her anger. What *were* these men doing here? Why were they being so secretive about it?

"Are you spying on people?" she asked boldly. It didn't seem as though there was anyone about to even spy *on*. The street was empty except for a few labourers passing through on their way to work, and a shopkeeper several doors down opening up for the day.

The detective winced. "We are not spying. We are investigating. It's entirely different."

Janey mulled that over. "What are you investigating, then?"

She did not yet trust them entirely – they were, after all, invaders on her territory who seemed to be poking their noses into something that was none of their business.

Mr. Holmes smiled. "We are investigating a ghost. But

we mustn't stand here. There is a tea shop on Commercial Street that we passed by not an hour ago. Have you lunched? Perhaps you will allow us to treat you to a meal. We can speak safely once we're out of sight."

Janey's stomach growled, loudly. Lunch? She hadn't even had breakfast! She was nodding before she even had a chance to think about it. For now, the needs of her stomach outweighed her confusion about the strange men's motives. Following Mr. Holmes and Dr. Watson out of the passage into Pearl Street, Janey suddenly felt sorry that Rose was at school, missing out on this treat. The girl needed a good, free meal as urgently as Janey did herself – if not even more.

The three of them walked back up to Commercial Street and into Mrs. Smithe's teahouse. At this hour, it was fairly empty. The dock workers loaded and unloaded ships all day, the housemaids hired out by the day, even neighbourhood pickpockets were already hard at work. Few had time for a leisurely mid-day meal. The shop was quiet, but also warm and bright, and more importantly - full of delicious smells.

They found an empty table tucked into the back. Dr. Watson ordered an extravagant meal - tea, milk, beef sandwiches, scones and jam, and a plate of iced cakes. Janey fell upon the food, too hungry to care much for politeness. She started with the sandwiches in between gulps of milk, and worked her way through to the cakes.

When there was nothing left on the table but crumbs and three half-finished cups of tea, she finally looked up. Holmes and Watson were looking down at her with amusement.

"That seems to have been acceptable?" Watson smiled.

"Yes, thank you," Janey replied. "It was very good."

Holmes snorted. "Are you quite finished?" he asked. "Are you sure you wouldn't care for another sandwich?"

"No, thank you, sir." Now that she'd eaten, Janey remembered her manners. She was also growing used to Holmes's slightly sarcastic manner of speaking. It offended her less than it had the first time.

"Very well, then, Janey Wiggins. I said that I had a proposition for you, and here it is. I am, as I mentioned earlier, a consulting detective – the only one in the world!"

Janey looked confused. "A consulting detective?"

She knew what detectives were, knew that some worked for the police to solve crimes, but these men did not look like police officers to her.

"That means that people come to him – to us – when they have a mystery that they need help solving. Sometimes we help the police, other times our clients are just ordinary people who need help unravelling strange happenings," Dr. Watson explained. "Holmes has an extraordinary genius for getting to the bottom of things. I am his friend and helper."

"Oh!" Janey exclaimed. "So, you were in the alley investigating a case for a client?"

"Exactly," Holmes said.

"Ha!" Janey exclaimed. "I *knew* you didn't have a friend there!"

Holmes's face flickered with annoyance. "What gave us away?"

Janey thought for a moment. She had known so instinctively that Holmes and Watson were outsiders that it was difficult for her to articulate her reasons.

"Your clothes," she said eventually. "You're so well-dressed, and your clothes are so new. You don't dress the way people around here do. People like you aren't friends with people like us."

At that, Dr. Watson looked sad – but Janey knew that it was true.

"And also," she continued, "I've never seen you before! If you were such good friends with someone around here, I'd definitely have seen you," she finished confidently.

"Aha!" Holmes exclaimed. "That expertise is *exactly* what we need."

"Oh, no," Janey said. Her stomach sank. "I'm not an expert in anything. I'm just a street girl. I'm not even in school."

He turned to her, and looked searchingly into her eyes. "Janey Wiggins," he said, "there are many different kinds of expertise. Now, can we trust you?"

"Of course you can!" Janey exclaimed. "I keep my promises and I know when to hold my tongue. I give you my word on that, at least."

Holmes and Watson looked at each other for a moment as if they were having a silent conversation. Finally, they nodded slightly at each other. Holmes turned back to her.

"Alright, Janey. You seem like a smart, strong, trustworthy girl. We could use your help in a very strange and difficult case. What do you say – are you in?"

Janey thought that she'd never heard anything so exciting in her life; certainly not since she had left school. She didn't know how she could possibly help, but desperately wanted to try. She nodded vigorously.

"Excellent." Holmes rubbed his hands together in satisfaction. "Watson!" he cried. "Where is your notebook? We must tell Miss Wiggins all about it."

Chapter Eight

Dr. Watson reached into the inside pocket of his jacket and removed a small, leather-bound notebook. Janey watched closely as he leafed through it. It was full of scribbled notes and what looked like an occasional diagram and sketched map.

"Watson is my chronicler," Holmes explained to Janey. "He takes careful notes of each of our cases. His assistance is invaluable to me."

Watson smiled. "Aha!" he exclaimed. "Here is the entry." He marked a place with his finger.

"Read it out, would you?" Holmes asked. "It is always helpful to hear the facts of the case, such as they are." He turned to Janey. "That is your first lesson in detecting. Always start with the facts."

She nodded solemnly. That was just common sense, wasn't it?

Dr. Watson began to read:

Last Sunday, a man showed up at our door unannounced at nine o'clock in the morning. He introduced himself as a Mr. Erwin Roberts of Pearl Street and said that he had urgent need of our advice. He was pale and trembling, and appeared to be frightened half out of his wits. I calmed him down as best I could, and got him seated by the fire with a cup of tea beside him. He then told us his story. "I was walking home from work last night, very late – after midnight," he began. "It had been a very long and tiring day for me, and I was looking forward to my dinner and my bed. My house is at the end of Pearl Street. I must walk the whole length of it, with its run-down old buildings and dark passages, to get home."

"That," Holmes interrupted, "is where you found us loitering, of course." Watson continued:

"I always hurry down that street," Mr. Roberts said. "It's a dark and lonely stretch. If one is given to imaginings, well—" he shuddered. "I hurried, then, and tucked my head down and thought of my cozy home waiting for me, just a few minutes away. Gentlemen, I promise you that I don't know what it was that caused me to stop halfway down the street. It was as if I had been called by a silent voice, or touched by an invisible hand. In any case, I stopped dead in my tracks right where Selby Passage branches off Pearl Street. At that instant, the moon came out from behind a cloud and I turned my face up to look at it. As I did, I suddenly became aware that a face was watching me out of one of the upper windows of the building facing me. I don't know what it was about that face, Mr. Holmes, but it seemed to send a chill right down my back. I was some little way off, so that I could not make out the features, but there was something uncanny about it. I moved quickly forward to get a nearer view. But as I did so, the face started up and disappeared so suddenly that it seemed to have been plucked away into the darkness. I don't know how long I stood in that alley with my blood turning icy in my veins. I could not tell if the face were that of a man or a woman – or even a child. Indeed, I could not swear that it had been human!

But its color was what had impressed me most - a livid, chalky white, with something set and rigid about it which was shockingly unnatural. It had something of the grave about it, I swear to you.

"The man was terrified," Dr. Watson told Janey, pausing in his reading. "As he told his story, he began to tremble again – just at the memory of what he had seen."

"Naturally," Holmes interjected, "we suspected that his imagination might have run away with him – that he had been seeing things, hallucinating in his extreme fatigue. It does sometimes happen, as you may know."

Janey did not know. But she supposed it made sense that if people dreamed extraordinary things at night, a very, very tired person might do so while awake, as well.

"We talked with Mr. Roberts at great length, however," Watson went on. "He turned out to be as level-headed and unimaginative as any man either of us had met. Neither was he so exhausted that he would be prone to seeing strange ghosts at windows."

"*Ghosts?*" Janey breathed. She was a sensible girl; she did not believe in such things. Surely neither would Mr. Holmes and Dr. Watson?

"That is the word Mr. Roberts used to describe the figure he saw," Holmes said. "He was quite insistent. It could not have been a ghost, however, as they do not exist."

"Of course not," Janey agreed. She didn't believe in anything as foolish as ghosts.

"But still, he saw *something* in the window that night," Holmes said. "Something that petrified him, and had him trembling like a leaf many hours later. He has asked us – Dr. Watson and I, that is – to find out what it was that he saw."

Janey nodded. If something like that had ever happened to her, she would want to get to the bottom of it, too. "Why do you need my help?" she asked.

"Ah, Janey," Holmes said, sitting back in his chair and looking at her with his piercing, intelligent eyes. "You have certain advantages that we do not."

"Like what?" Janey looked at herself - a poor street girl in a grubby, threadbare dress. Then she looked at Holmes and Watson - wealthy, educated, brilliant. What advantages could she offer that they could not obtain on their own?

"Your superior knowledge of this neighbourhood, for one thing," Holmes replied. "You were perceptive enough to recognize that Dr. Watson and I were strangers here, and that our cover story was a lie. You read people very well, Janey."

Janey flushed. Was Holmes mocking her? Anyone would have been able to see what she had seen. There was nothing special about her.

"Another point in your favour is your size. I am a tall fellow, Janey, and so is Dr. Watson. It can be difficult to investigate some cases because we are so obvious in our appearance. But you! You're small and quick. You can get into places we would never be able to access."

"That's nothing!" Janey said, all in a rush. She couldn't

bear to hear this false praise for another second. "I'm a poor street girl – you said so yourself. I don't even go to school." She hung her head. "I'm nothing."

Holmes's fist slammed down on the table, and Janey jumped. She looked up into eyes that burned like tiny suns. He leaned forward and said intently, "Take your weakness, and forge it into strength. Take your powerlessness and use it to your advantage. You're a clever girl. *Use* it."

Janey wasn't sure she understood. Holmes started at her intently for a moment more, then shrugged his shoulders and sat back. The moment had passed.

In a more conversational tone, he said, "No one ever pays attention to children, have you noticed? Young girls, especially. *They* think you are nothing, perhaps – all but invisible. That is their mistake, and a mistake is a weakness that you can use. You have the freedom of the streets at your feet. No one will ever give you a second glance. I am, in fact, quite jealous when I think of it."

Janey smiled a little. It was true – no one ever looked at her. No one even moved out of her way when she walked down the street. She was practically invisible, except to her mother and her friends.

"Miss Wiggins," Holmes continued, "we require someone to watch the house at 54 Pearl Street, right opposite to Selby Passage, and report any unusual happenings back to us. That is the house where Mr. Roberts saw his 'ghost.' As you observed, yourself, Watson and I stick out like a sore thumb in this neighbourhood. If we try to keep watch again, we'll only draw more attention to ourselves and risk setting our mysterious 'ghost' off. So, will you work for us?"

Chapter Nine

For a moment, Janey thought she must have misunderstood the detective.

"Work for you? Does that mean," she asked hesitantly, "Would I be a detectivelike you?"

Holmes looked at her, seriously. There was no trace of his earlier laughter. "Do you know what an 'irregular' is?" he asked.

Janey shook her head.

"The word has many meanings," Holmes said, "but for our purposes, 'irregulars' are people who don't officially belong to any group or profession, but do the job anyway. They are not one of the 'regular' workforce, but work alongside it. You are not a detective. Not yet," he added, when her face fell. "It takes many years of study, work and experience to become one. One day, when you are much older, perhaps you will be. Perhaps you'll be the greatest detective London has ever seen!" His eyes flashed and Janey felt a spark of excitement lodge itself in her belly right where her hunger pains used to be.

"But for now," he continued, "you will be an apprentice. An irregular. Agreed?"

Janey nodded. A small smile grew on her face. She was going to be an irregular! She was already swelling with pride at the thought.

"Excellent!" Holmes said. "Here are our terms: we will

pay you a shilling for every clue you bring us, for I believe in paying people what they are worth. Two shillings for a major discovery, and a crown at the successful conclusion of a case."

Janey felt her heart thump in her chest. She'd never earned that much money in her life.

Dr. Watson held up a cautionary finger. "We have some rules, Janey."

Holmes looked surprised. "Do we?" he asked.

All at once, Dr. Watson looked very cross indeed.

"Holmes!" he barked. "You cannot expect a child to run the same risks that we do in our work. We *do* have some rules." He stared hard at the detective, as if inviting him to challenge him.

Holmes was silent.

Janey looked between the two men curiously. They were so very different from each other. How did they get along so well?

"The first rule," Dr. Watson continued, turning to Janey, "is that you must only *ever* observe. You must never, ever approach anyone involved in the investigation. We do not want to accidentally mix you up with dangerous criminals. You are to watch from a safe distance. That is all. Do you understand?"

Janey nodded. The rule made sense. She suspected her mother would agree with it.

"The second rule is that you must always come to us

at the very first sign of trouble. Here is our card." He handed her a small, cardboard rectangle with their names and an address printed on in in block letters.

"221B Baker Street," she read aloud.

"You can read!" Holmes exclaimed, sounding pleased.

"Of *course* I can read!" she huffed indignantly. "Just because I'm not in school now doesn't mean I'm a fool! I studied hard until I was 10 years old!"

"Oh, yes, you're very accomplished." Holmes was back to his sarcastic self, but Janey barely noticed.

"Should you ever feel uncertain or unsafe, come to Baker Street. We will help you," Watson repeated.

Again, Janey nodded. "I will," she said.

"Good. Your first priority must always be your own safety and wellbeing. No investigation is worth harming yourself." He winked at her. "That's a lesson Holmes himself has not yet learned."

Holmes simply rolled his eyes.

"The final rule," Watson went on, "is that you must be discrete. Our investigations are often very private and sensitive in nature. We must always keep our clients' information between ourselves."

"*Obviously*," Janey and Holmes said at the same time.

Watson laughed delightedly. "You two make quite the pair."

Holmes snorted in amusement. Even Janey felt the

corner of her mouth turn upward.

"Now that Dr. Watson has thoroughly cautioned you," Holmes said, "I believe it is my turn to speak. There are certain principles of detective work, Janey – rules that you must learn and practice if you wish to become a detective yourself. These are principles that I live by, and you would do well to do the same."

Janey suddenly wished she had a notebook like Watson's. She opened her eyes very wide and focused on committing every word to memory. This was far better than *Ernest Keen*!

"I have already given you the first principle. Do you remember?"

Janey nodded. "Always start with the facts."

"Excellent!" Holmes praised. "Your memory is sound, and I am pleased to hear it. The three principles are as follows:

1. Always start with the facts. Without a clear grounding, one can make no progress.

2. Observe the details. Sometimes the smallest, most insignificant detail might be the clue that solves the case.

3. No matter how much we want the fantastic to be real, the simplest explanation is usually the right one."

This made good sense to Janey. She nodded, thinking about Mr. Roberts and the Pearl Street ghost. How might she apply these principles in this case?

By the time Holmes had finished giving his

instructions, their meal was over and it was time to depart. Janey and Dr. Watson followed him out into the street where he turned and held out his hand. This time Janey shook it warmly.

"We have an arrangement, then. Good luck, Janey. We'll see you soon at Baker Street. You must come the very instant you have information to report."

"I will. Goodbye, Mr. Holmes. Goodbye, Dr. Watson. Thank you." She turned away and had made it halfway up the street already when she heard hurried footsteps behind her. She turned, and there was Dr. Watson, pressing something into her hand.

"For you and your friends," he said with a friendly wink. "Get another good meal into you. We can't have our associates starving, can we?" Then he ran down the street again, following at Holmes' heels.

Janey looked down. A shiny sixpence rested on her palm.

Chapter Ten

Janey walked the short distance up Commercial Street towards her home, thinking hard. She clutched the sixpence tightly in her fist. She'd done odd jobs to earn a shilling or two here and there, and her mother had occasionally given her a handful of coins to buy food or milk, but she'd never had so much money of her own before. Even when she'd gone with her mother to sell flowers at Covent Garden, she'd turned over all of her earnings to her mother every night so she could pay for their food or rent. She squeezed the coin so tightly she could feel the edges of it digging into her palm.

She'd agreed to watch the house at Pearl Street and to be Holmes's irregular detective. But Janey couldn't watch it every minute of the day and night, could she? Surely Holmes would not be expecting her to do that! Her mother would be frantic with worry if she were out later than the midnight bells.

But what if something happened while she wasn't there! The ghost had first appeared late at night – wasn't it likely to keep late hours? Janey desperately wanted to impress Holmes. She had to think of a way to keep the house under watch at all times – even when she couldn't be there herself.

Janey stopped in her tracks. She had a lot of friends! Maybe Dr. Watson had given her a hint when he handed her the money, telling her to use it to feed her friends. She could recruit them! Between the lot of them, they could easily watch the house. Janey could work out a schedule with her friends to keep it under their observation at all times - she could watch

49

during the daylight hours when her mother was working. Of course, she would give them a fair share of Holmes's pay, too.

Rose was at school during the day, but she could surely manage the evenings; she could even give the extra money to her brother to keep his mind off of the soap factory. Janey shuddered. She'd do almost anything to keep the girl out of the factories.

If she took day watch and Rose took evenings, who could watch during the night? Janey wracked her brain. It would have to be someone older – someone whose parents wouldn't be looking out for them, and who had enough sense to evade the Vigilance Committee. Then it struck her.

"Emily!" Janey thought in a flash of inspiration. Her cousin Emily was a big girl of sixteen years. She would be the perfect person for the job.

I can do this, Janey thought excitedly. *We* can do this!

With a plan firmly in place, Janey's slow, contemplative pace became a cheerful skip. For the first time in a very long time, she was looking forward to the future. She didn't know what it would bring, but with Holmes and Watson in the picture, she knew it would be an adventure.

She stopped suddenly. In the large window of the dressmaker's shop to her left, tucked in behind a rack of gaudy new fabrics, was a large straw bonnet. It was a strange thing to be seen in the middle of a London winter, its broad-brimmed edges meant to keep the sun off one's face, trimmed with bright ribbon. Janey thought how fine it would look on her mother; how it would draw customers to her when she plied her trade at Covent Garden. Why, in that bonnet and a pretty new cotton dress, she'd look like summer itself and no customer would be able to resist her fragrant bouquets. What Janey would give to be able to buy something so fine – so frivolous – for her mother. She pressed her nose up against the glass, looking her fill at the beautiful hat. She wanted to remember every detail about it so that she could tell her mother all about it later that night.

Janey was so lost in her thoughts that she didn't hear the shop door rattle open, nor did she notice the shop assistant's approach. She didn't look up until she heard him shout.

"Oi! You! Clear off out of here! We don't need riffraff scaring off our good customers."

Janey's face blushed scarlet and she drew back from the window.

"I said get away!" He approached menacingly, shaking his fist.

Janey turned with a gasp and ran off, her eyes blurring with tears. Was she so insignificant, so unimportant, that she couldn't even stand on a public street and look at the goods displayed in a shop window? She blinked back her tears as she continued down the street. What was it that Holmes had said? "They think you are nothing. That is their mistake, and a mistake is a weakness that you can use."

Well then, she thought, *use it I shall*! She would show them. She would show everyone who thought she was nothing, who ignored and belittled and mocked her just how clever she could be!

Chapter Eleven

The next morning, Janey woke with the sun. A new feeling of excitement and anticipation washed over her.

Her mother had risen when it was still dark and asked Janey to accompany her to the flower stall that day, but Janey pretended to have a headache. Her mother only sighed and kissed her cheek.

"I don't believe you, you know," she said softly, but she squeezed her hand and told her to stay in bed for the day all the same. When Janey finally rose, she had already left for her long walk to Covent Garden, but there was a small, cheery fire in the grate to warm the room. Her mother had left a glass of fresh milk and a half-loaf of the baker's bread on the little table beside their bed.

Janey hadn't told her about her new employment or about her plans. Her mother hadn't even wanted her to go to school! The girl was certain she'd forbid her from working for Holmes were she to know. Her mother would be too suspicious of their motives, too worried about Janey's safety to allow it. Better to keep it quiet. Something to hold close to her chest like a ray of hope – something of her own.

Lying on the floor where her mother had dropped it when she'd fallen asleep the night before was a newspaper, two days old and crinkled with use. It had passed through many hands before her mother had managed to snag it for their entertainment, but Janey had been too absorbed in her own mind to be interested in reading it. She pretended to be exhausted and curled up in bed with her thoughts while her mother read silently to herself. She thought about Rose and Emily, wondering how to explain exactly what she wanted them to do.

She picked up the paper and her milk, going over to sit at the dingy window overlooking the street. After her feast the day before, her simple breakfast was disappointing. She ripped her bread in half, wrapping one piece in a handkerchief to save for Rose. She needed it more than Janey – the poor girl would be starving.

Absently, she leafed through the newspaper on her lap. The headlines were old, of course – she'd heard all the important bits on the street days ago, but there was always the possibility she'd chance upon some new tidbit or detail that she could share with her friends.

As she drank her milk, she began to read. Nothing much caught her interest until she got to an inside page and saw the lurid headline: *DEATH IN THE CITY! ILLNESS HAUNTS THE EAST END!* She pulled the paper to her with a pang as she realized that more people than usual had been falling ill to the dreaded tuberculosis. Everyone in the neighbourhood knew someone with TB. A feeling of unease, a growing sense of worry, was beginning to drift through the area.

The article ran,

The weekly tally of new cases of tuberculosis continues to soar in the East End of London, causing great concern among the city's population. There were almost 1,200 deaths in January of last year when the disease was under control. This January's total was almost double that number, making it the deadliest outbreak of tuberculosis the city has seen in well over a decade. The East End has been particularly affected with the majority of new cases being identified there. Doctors suspect the area is particularly susceptible to new infections because of the high rates of poverty: small rooms, shared beds, poor sanitation, and crowded conditions, all of which allow the disease to spread more easily. To avoid infecting others, patients must be quarantined in isolation until the infectious stage of the illness has passed. Doctors are calling for stricter monitoring of these patients.

Janey shuddered. She knew several people who had been ill. Some of them had recovered from the fearful, bloody coughs that wracked their bodies, leaving them breathless, weak, exhausted, while others had not been so lucky. Tuberculosis was a terrible illness. Aside from rest, there was no real treatment for it. She thought of Rose's mother, locked away in the Infectious Diseases Hospital until she was well again. Rose wasn't allowed to see her. In fact, they only had a vague notion of where the hospital even was.

Janey hoped with all her might that Rose's mother would return well and healthy.

A terrible thought struck her. What would become of Janey if her own mother were to get infected? Fear swept through her like a cold wave. She could never make it on her own. Not even with Holmes and Watson's pay. She'd never have enough money to pay for the room, let alone food or anything else.

Heartsick, she crumpled the newspaper into a tight ball and threw it into the corner. Her mother would scold her for the waste - surely someone else would want to read it. For the moment Janey didn't care.

She stood suddenly. There was no point sitting alone in her room, wasting the daylight hours – not when Holmes had entrusted her with an important investigation. She had work to do.

Quickly tying her hair back, Janey slipped on her boots, pulled her shawl around her shoulders, and was out the door in less than a minute.

Chapter Twelve

The sun was bright, but the air was cold for a London winter. Janey's breath fogged the air in front of her when she stepped out onto the street. As she walked, she remembered what Holmes had told her.

Truly, no one paid any attention to her at all. She passed at least ten people within the distance of a single block and not one of them even glanced at her. Almost as if she *were* invisible. Janey was tempted to stick her tongue out at the shopkeepers opening their stalls just to see if they'd notice her, but instead she tucked her head down and hurried along. Irregulars, she thought, should not draw attention to themselves. She wanted to get back to Pearl Street as soon as possible, but there were a few errands to run first.

Her first job was to find her cousin Emily and convince her that taking the night watch would be worth her while.

Emily was a maid in a large house on Mile End Road, right on the very edge of the East End. She "lived in," which meant she shared a bed with another servant girl, and worked awfully hard all day keeping the house clean and tidy for her employers. Janey had visited her there before when Emily had her half-day off. It was back-breaking work, she told Janey – she worked hard scrubbing floors and beating carpets, making beds and doing all the other hard labour of the house from the early hours of the morning through nightfall. Her hands were always cracked and bleeding from the hot, soapy water. But what choice did she have? Her mother had six other children to support, and Emily was old enough to make her own way in the world. A very demanding job and a very tiny, shared bed were far better than a miserable life on the streets. Janey knew there were people like that, people without money or a roof over their heads. She was grateful that her family, at least, was better off than that.

It took her just thirty minutes to walk to Emily's house. Ignoring the front door, Janey stepped around to the rear of the house and knocked lightly on the kitchen door. Emily would be at her work by now, and Janey had no wish to cause trouble with her employers. As she stood on the doorstep shivering, through an upper window she heard a woman coughing and coughing. Somewhere, a baby was crying. Further off down the street she heard two girls singing a skipping song.

The door swung open. A pale, curly-haired girl wearing a plain dress with an apron poked her head out just as Janey was about to knock again. The girl broke into a wide grin.

"Janey!" Emily exclaimed in surprise. "I never thought to see you standing on our doorstep first thing in the morning!" Her voice, for all her excitement, was hushed, and she looked behind her guiltily.

"Can you talk?" Janey asked.

"The cook has me peeling potatoes and carrots, but she's not here just now. I think I can sneak away for a few minutes. Can we go outside?" she asked quietly.

"Of course," Janey said. Emily slipped through the door. They snuck away a little ways, stopping by a gate that stood open behind the outhouse. There, they could talk for a few minutes without being observed by anyone in the house.

It was good to see Emily again, Janey thought. For all that they lived so close, Janey had seen her only a handful of times since she'd gone into service. *She does look tired*, Janey thought. The hard work was taking a toll on her. Emily looked wan, thinner than she had before.

Emily had always been Janey's favourite. She'd never had an older sister, and Emily often filled that role, sewing clothes for Erna Keen from scraps she'd saved, and playing with Janey when no one else had time to.

Emily was kind – a good, kind soul without a scrap of self-interest. Janey admired her more than anyone else she knew.

There had been a terrible accident when Emily was Janey's age. Janey herself had been too young to remember it, but one day when Emily was home alone, caring for her younger siblings, the family's kerosene lamp had exploded in her face when she'd tried to light it. She'd managed to put the fire out, keeping the younger children safe, but Emily, herself, had been terribly hurt by the flames. It took her months to heal. She'd had burns over her arms and hands, and one side of her face, as well. Those burns had turned to livid, red scars.

To Janey, though, her cousin would always be beautiful. Such misfortune would turn some people inward: make them sad, sour or cruel. But it had only made Emily kinder, made her want to help every living creature who suffered. Janey loved her fiercely.

"How are you, Janey?" Emily asked. "How's your mother?"

"We're well, we're well," Janey answered impatiently. The longer she was away from Pearl Street, the more anxious she became. What if the ghost had reappeared? What if she missed it? Would Holmes ever want to employ her again?

"Listen, Emily. I have a favour to ask you. It's a big one, and it's sort of a secret. Can I trust you to hold your tongue?"

Emily's eyes widened. Janey had never spoken to her so seriously before. "You know you can."

Janey nodded. She did know, but she wanted to underscore the seriousness of her request.

"Listen, Emily. Something happened to me yesterday. You're never going to believe this..." She went on to relate the events of the night before. Even to her own ears, it sounded like an incredibly far-fetched tale - the poor and lonely street child swept up into the exciting world of a mysterious detective. She wasn't sure she would believe it either, if it hadn't happened to her!

Emily listened with her astonished eyes growing wider by the minute. She didn't interrupt until Janey was done with her story. Then, the girl leaned back and whistled lowly.

"Blimey!" she exclaimed. "The strangest things do happen to you!"

Janey burst out laughing. It really was very strange. It was strange, and wonderful, and entirely exciting!

"To begin with," Emily said seriously, "I don't like to hear about you wandering the streets and taking meals or money from strange men. It isn't safe! You know better, Janey!"

"But Emily-" Janey couldn't believe her cousin was lecturing her about safety. "You've no need to worry! Holmes and Watson are good, decent men. They were very kind to me!" If Emily were to decide this venture was too dangerous for a young girl – if she were to tell her mother about it! – Janey realized with horror that her adventure would be over before it truly began. To her dismay, Janey felt tears pricking at her eyes. She broke off as Emily waved her concern away.

"You're lucky I always keep my word, Janey-girl," Emily said, nudging her with an elbow. "And you're awfully lucky about who you chanced to quite literally run into last night."

"Oh?" She looked at her blankly.

"Have you not heard of- Good lord, Janey! What have you done with yourself since you left school? You used to be such a know-it-all!"

Janey stuck her tongue out at her.

"Hang on," Emily said and darted quickly back into the house. She returned a few seconds later carrying a newspaper. "Look there," she said, pointing to a column near the top of the first page. "This is from last week – and it's just the latest."

Jane read aloud:

SHERLOCK HOLMES FOILS MYSTERIOUS BANK ROBBERY

Last night two escaped prisoners made a daring attempt to rob the National Bank in Old Broad Street. The bank had just received an unusually large delivery of gold in addition to the almost half a million pounds in its safe. It is unknown how the thieves discovered this, however, they would certainly have carried off their plan successfully had it not been for the brilliant and swift intervention of Mr. Holmes, who caught the thieves red-handed and pursued them as they attempted to flee. He and his colleague, Dr. Watson, managed to catch them before they could even make it to the street and held them until the police arrived. Our city is once again indebted to Mr. Holmes and his exceptional detective work.

This time it was Janey who whistled in surprise.

"He's famous, then?" she asked tentatively.

"Very!" Emily answered. "He's in the papers all the time! I can't believe you've never noticed."

Janey shrugged. Since she left school, her reading habits had become sporadic. She'd rather read a book than a newspaper, anyway, but those were hard to come by.

"In any case, I'm relieved," Emily went on. "You've managed to find the most trustworthy employer in the city. Well done, you!"

"He won't be my employer for long if I don't do the work he asked me to. I need your help, Emily! I can't possibly watch the house at night. Mother would worry herself sick if

I missed my curfew, and Rose is still too little. Could you? Could you slip away after dark and keep an eye on it for me? For us? Rose and I will take the day and evening watches, and if you take the night, we can divide our pay equally between us. You're the only one old enough to be out at night!"

Emily's face clouded a bit. "I might be able to manage it for a night or two," she said, "but I really can't risk it for longer than that. If my employers found out, I could lose my job here – and I can't let that happen."

Janey was flooded with relief. "That's perfect, Emily!" she assured her. "Just two nights. Just to see what happens. Maybe we can solve the case before then!"

Emily smiled indulgently. "Maybe we can."

"The only thing is, the Vigilance Committee has been getting ugly recently. You'll have to avoid them as best you can. If they give you any trouble for being out at night, say that you're a respectable maid on an errand for your master."

Emily snorted. "I think I can give those dolts the slip," she said confidently. "No worries there, but thanks for the warning."

They arranged to meet that night at the house just before Janey's midnight curfew.

As she turned to leave, Janey hesitated. "Are you hungry, Emily?"

Emily shrugged. "I'm *always* hungry, aren't I? Always tired, always hungry." She smiled a wavering sort of smile.

"Dr. Watson gave me some money. He said I should

buy food for myself and my friends. I'll bring us all some supper tonight, shall I? Some fried fish and baked potatoes?"

Emily smiled. "Lovely! This job is paying off already."

Janey kissed her cheek and took her leave.

She did not expect her next stop to be as pleasant. She set her feet on a path they knew well – knew, but had avoided for two whole years. Rose should be at the Charity School by now, waiting with the other children for the morning bell to ring and for lessons to begin. The usual bitter taste of jealousy filled her mouth when she thought of it, but today, for the first time, Janey had something else on her mind.

She had known Rose for most of her life. They'd met years before, when Rose was barely out of nappies and just starting to speak in full sentences. In those days, they'd lived in the same building; their rooms were beside each other. Sometimes Janey would hear the little girl crying or fussing through the walls and would go collect her and entertain her for a few hours, much to the delight of her mother. Although their mothers had moved to different buildings, Rose and Janey had remained close. They'd grown older together, running about in the streets as if the East End was their own special playground. They watched out for each other. Rose was almost like a little sister to Janey. She hoped the girl had slept well the night before so that she could concentrate on her lessons.

As she walked up to the familiar iron railing that enclosed the school, Janey caught sight of Rose huddling against the side of the building with a group of girls her age.

She whistled their usual signal, and Rose looked up, brightening when she saw Janey. She jogged over to the fence and took Janey's hand between the railings.

"Janey!" the little girl said. "Is anything the matter? You never visit me here!"

For the second time that morning, Janey's heart warmed. She might be invisible to the world, but she was important to her friends and family - to Rose, to Emily, and certainly to her mother. She wasn't nothing.

She hastened to reassure Rose, to explain the details of her plan. As she talked, Janey pulled the bread in her handkerchief out of her pocket and passed it to Rose. The little girl took it gratefully, gulping it down as she listened.

"So, you are Holmes's irregular now?" she asked when Janey had finished.

"I am."

"Do you think - could I be *your* Irregular?" Rose asked.

Janey smiled. "We'll be Irregulars together, shall we? Meet me at Selby Passage after school."

Rose nodded eagerly.

Just then, the school bell rang. Rose turned and dashed to the entrance along with all the other rag-tag neighbourhood children. For once, Janey didn't feel sad or even jealous. She turned on her heel and walked out into a day that sparked with the promise of adventure.

Chapter Thirteen

Janey arrived at Pearl Street a little after 10 o'clock that morning. The street looked different in the winter sunlight. The strangeness and mystery of the night before had evaporated like mist. Workers passed up and down the lane – not many, but enough that there was always someone about. A man was whistling on his way to his job at the docks. A child hurried along, late for school. A daily maid's shoes clicked on the cobblestones as she made her way between jobs. These were the familiar sights and sounds of home to Janey.

She paused at the entrance to Selby Passage, kneeling as if to tie her shoelaces. She surveyed the scene critically, trying to observe details the way she knew Holmes did. The dirt and grime of the alley were a stark contrast against the beaming sun. The building walls lining the street were black with soot. The sewage running down the gutters let off an almost overpowering stink.

The house she was to observe - 54 Pearl Street - stood directly across from the passage where she'd found Holmes and Watson the day before. It provided the perfect cover for secret observation. Janey could duck into it and sink into the shadows. If she huddled against the brick wall near the mouth of the alley and drew her dark shawl around her, no one would ever even know she was there. She stood, took a last look around, and did just that.

She pulled her shawl around her, shivering. She hadn't realized the ground would be so cold, but at least, tucked away in the passage, there were no puddles of sewage to contend with. Her breath formed clouds in front of her face. She pulled the shawl even closer, pulling it up over her head, leaving just a small slit for her eyes to peek out of. She doubted anyone would see her. Although workers used Pearl Street during the day, few if any turned into Selby Passage. If anyone did happen to walk by, they would just assume Janey was another street beggar, stopped to rest in a quiet corner. There were so many beggars in the East End, no one would think anything of it.

Through her shawl, Janey could see the house perfectly. It was a run-down affair - narrow, squeezed in between two larger buildings on either side. It was made of sloping, crumbling brick and rotting wood. There was a single entrance - a door that someone, long ago, had painted a cheery green. The paint was peeling, the wood caked in years of dust and grime. "Cheery" was the last word that came to Janey's mind as she looked at it. The house was a single story with a tiny attic window over the front door.

She stared hard at that little attic window. That must be where the ghost had been! Try as she might, Janey could see nothing unusual about it at all; no clue that she could offer Holmes. It was an ordinary window, shut fast against the winter cold. It appeared to be covered with heavy drapes, heavy enough that Janey could not see through them. The single downstairs window was similarly fashioned – for privacy, Janey assumed. No one liked to have strangers looking in on them while they ate their breakfast.

In short, Janey was staring at a house that was no

different from dozens, hundreds, maybe even thousands, in this area of London. She sighed with irritation, and then a minute later she laughed at herself. Had she expected the ghost to appear the instant she arrived? Of course not! She must be clever, like a detective. She must be patient. What was it that Holmes had told her? *Always start with the facts.*

Very well, then, she told herself, *I will have to wait for the facts to present themselves.*

She waited and watched.

Chapter Fourteen

Janey waited and waited, sitting in her little corner of the passage, wrapped against the cold.

She sat there for so long that her backside went sore, then numb. So long that her stomach began to growl. So long that she almost began to nod off. But Janey was a stubborn girl, and she was determined. Through all of her body's small protests, she sat and watched.

Nothing happened. There was no sign of life from the house. No one moved within. Sometimes Janey's mind would wander off into a daydream. She'd think about what Rose could be doing at school or imagined stories of Ernest Keen's latest adventure. Each time, she caught herself and shook her head crossly, pulling herself out of the daydreams, returning her full attention to the house.

A beggar man came down the street. Janey watched idly as he knocked on each door in turn, asking despairingly for a crust of bread or bit of cheese. Anything to "keep his body and soul together."

Most of the people who opened their doors shooed him away with a curse or a fist. He was still empty handed when he at last made it to number 54. Janey watched with interest as he knocked on the door.

There was no answer at first. As the man raised his hand to knock again, the door swung open and a large woman in a long apron appeared. She had a kind, open face, but her eyes darted up and down the street nervously.

"Please, madam," Janey heard the beggar say. "Can you spare a crust for a desperate man?"

The woman's eyes softened. She shook her head and raised her hand in a gesture of incomprehension, whispering something under her breath. She took his arm and drew him into the house with a smile.

"Thank you, madam! Thanks with all my heart," the beggar man was saying as the woman ushered him in.

The woman merely patted his shoulder and closed the door behind him.

Janey was dumbstruck. She knew from experience that most people would do nothing for a person in desperate need – certainly not if the person was a stranger, and a beggar to boot. She'd seen the truth of this as the man had walked away with empty hands and an even emptier stomach from all the other houses on the street. For some reason, this woman had been kind; she'd treated him almost like a friend.

Her heart warmed to the woman.

Janey sat still, quivering with excitement now instead of with cold. She wondered what was going on inside the house.

Twenty minutes later, the door opened again and the beggar man departed. Janey strained to see into the house as the door opened, but the man stepped out and the door quickly shut behind him again. He was wearing a different coat than before: his ratty, holey old garment had been exchanged for a warm-looking wool greatcoat. It was old and unfashionable, but it appeared to be warm and in good condition.

She looked back at the house, thinking hard.

Suddenly she knew what she should do. That man had seen the inside of the house! He had spoken to the people who lived there! She couldn't let him disappear without talking to him.

"He is my first witness!" Janey whispered to herself as she leapt up and tore after the man. He had made his way down the street already.

"Sir!" Janey cried, trying to catch his attention. "Sir!"

But the man – dirty, poor, and all but invisible to his fellows – had not been called "sir" in so many years that he didn't turn around, didn't even slow his steps.

He was halfway down Pearl Street now, and Janey was desperate.

She dashed up to the man and did the first thing she could think of to make him stop - she caught hold of his sleeve and tugged impatiently on it.

"Sir," she said again. "Please."

Startled, the man stopped walking and turned to look at her with suspicion in his eyes. "What is it?" he asked gruffly.

"If you please, sir," Janey gasped. "Where did you get that coat?"

The man drew back from her angrily. "What business

is that of yours?" he demanded. He had a booming voice.

"It's – it's not my business. But please, it's very important!" She had to make him understand.

The man flushed scarlet and abruptly shoved her, square in the chest. Janey staggered backwards, then fell painfully onto the cobblestones. She gasped with shock and pain. By the time she could gather her wits again, the beggar man was striding down the street, quickly lost amongst the throng of people who had turned to stare at her.

Janey winced – with pain and embarrassment. She was doing an extremely poor job of silent observation. Would the people living at number 54 be hearing this? Could they be watching her right now?

Almost unwillingly, her eyes darted quickly back to the house, as if she might catch sight of the kind woman peering out of the door or peeking from behind the thickly curtained window.

But what she saw instead made her blood run cold.

Hovering in the attic window, a face looked down on the street.

Janey immediately understood what Mr. Roberts had said when he described the ghost to Holmes. It did indeed look inhuman - far too pale, too white, somehow twisted in a way that did not look natural. Worst of all, sunken deep in its head, there were dark black hollows where eyes should be. It slowly turned to look at her. Her heart pounded in her chest.

Janey felt a scream rising in her throat that she

swallowed down with difficulty. Those black holes drilled terror into her very soul. Her body felt doused with ice water. She began to shake.

The ghost moved with a jerky motion towards the edge of the window. Coming closer. Its eyes – or at least, the holes where its eyes should have been – remained locked with hers.

For the second time in two days, Janey saw stars swirling before her eyes. She blinked furiously, and her vision cleared.

She looked up again to the window where the ghost had been. It was empty, and the curtain had been pulled back once more into place.

Chapter Fifteen

Janey and Rose sat huddled together at the entrance to Selby Passage. They'd shared the evening watch as Janey was reluctant to leave until she absolutely had to. There was a basket of food between them, purchased with the money from Dr. Watson. The girls were waiting impatiently for Emily to arrive before they ate.

When Rose had arrived after school, Janey had been glad of the company – and the support. They had sat together for the rest of the afternoon, talking quietly about what had happened. When Janey described her encounter with the beggar man, Rose had slapped her playfully on the hand.

"Janey!" she scolded. "Surely you knew better! Imagine what was going through his mind. He'd just been given a coat that was good enough to see him through many a winter. In his mind, you wanted to take it from him!"

Rose was right. Janey resolved to work harder at reading people and anticipating their thoughts. It would be an important skill to have in her detective work.

She had been so close to a clue, so close to the ghost! Now there was nothing.

Thinking about the ghost made her skin prickle all over again. Janey had thought she was far too sensible a girl to believe in ghosts, but the image danced behind her eyes every time she closed them.

"Rose," she asked hesitantly, "do you... Do you

believe in ghosts?"

The smaller girl looked up at her in surprise. "Course not!" she said bravely, but her voice was uncertain. "Everyone knows there's no such thing."

"You didn't see it, though," Janey said with a shudder. "Its eyes…" She stared hard at the house, her mind replaying the events of the day.

Rose huddled closer to her and tucked her little head into her shoulder. "You're scaring me now," she said quietly.

Janey was suddenly ashamed of herself. She had allowed herself to be frightened by specters of her own imagination. She'd seen *something* in that window, certainly, but it was ridiculous to fall back on childish fancies to explain it. Was she no better than Holmes's client? She must start with the facts in order to find a reasonable explanation.

She turned and took Rose's hand between her own.

"You're right, Rose," Janey said emphatically. "There's no such thing as ghosts. But there's *something* going on in that attic. I saw it with my own eyes. We are going to find out what it is."

Rose's little face set itself in a determined smile. "We will," she said. "I know we will."

Just then Emily arrived, sweeping around the corner, almost tripping over the two girls who were all but invisible in the dark passage. She let loose a muffled cry of surprise before a hand reached up, sharply pulling her down into their huddle.

"Hush, Emily!" Janey said sharply.

She smiled apologetically. "Sorry," she said. "I'm still learning this detective business, aren't I?"

As Janey filled her in on the events of the day, Rose opened their picnic basket and pulled out what looked like a magnificent feast to the three half-starved girls. She spread a clean handkerchief on the ground between them and on it placed the food that Janey had purchased earlier - big pieces of fresh fried fish, a whole baked potato for each, grapes, boiled eggs, and currant puddings.

The merchant had almost run Janey off, thinking her to be a thief, before seeing the shiny coin in her hand. She'd been mortified. With a pang, she realized that that's how the beggar man must have felt.

She'd have to think things through more carefully in the future.

The children fell to their dinner. With smacking lips and sighs of happiness they devoured it entirely. It wasn't often they had full bellies. This was a very special occasion – one to be savoured. At last, Emily looked up, licking a last bit of crumb from her fingers.

"If Holmes and Watson pay this well before we've even done any work, I reckon we're set for life!" she exclaimed.

Janey smiled lazily back at her. The long day of watching and waiting had caught up with her, and now that she'd eaten, she was ready to go home to her bed. Little Rose yawned beside her.

Suddenly, Janey stiffened. Her eyes were trained on the door of the house opposite. The last glow of the dusk was almost gone, just enough remained for her to see the door swing open. A man stepped out.

Janey shook off her lethargy, her mind clicking into gear. "Observe," she whispered to her friends, remembering Holmes's instructions. "Look for the details."

In the dying light, they saw the man look up and down the lane. He wore a felt cap and a cheap, but warm-looking coat. His trousers were worn and patched several times at the knees. It was too dark to see much of his face, but they could tell he had a full beard. He carried an empty sack over one arm.

The man stopped a few yards from the house and rifled around in his pockets for a moment, finally coming out with a pipe. Something white slipped out along with it and fluttered to the ground at his feet. The man didn't appear to notice. He lit his pipe and went on his way up Pearl Street.

In an instant, Janey was up and out of the passage.

"What is it?" Rose whispered eagerly as Janey came back into the passage.

"Emily, can you light a match?" Janey asked.

She did. The children huddled together around Janey's prize - a small piece of paper, folded over itself twice. Janey carefully unfolded it, smoothing the creases.

They stared at the paper in confusion. It looked like a

note, neat rows of figures written carefully in ink. But the writing made no sense! Letters were grouped together in ways they couldn't read, squiggles and lines randomly sprinkled across the page. Many of the markings didn't look like letters at all, but rather symbols that were unfamiliar to them.

"I don't understand," Rose said, wrinkling her nose.

"Oh!" Janey breathed, heart pumping in excitement. "It's a secret code." She'd seen similar clues in *Ernest Keen.*

"I don't know about that," Emily said, raising an eyebrow. "Seems to me it's much more likely to be a different language."

Janey rolled her eyes. "Don't you know *anything* about being a detective?" she asked scornfully. "There's always a secret code of some sort. And I'm going to crack it!"

Chapter Sixteen

That night, lying in her narrow bed, with her mother snoring softly beside her, Janey studied the slip of paper by the light of a single candle. No matter how she puzzled it out, she could not make heads or tails of it.

She tried all the codes and ciphers she knew – which were not many. There was a simple letter-replacement code she had used as a girl in school, passing little notes to her friends between lessons. She considered that possibility for some time, but nothing made sense.

She thought of a code she'd seen in a history book that used a system of non-letter symbols to make up words. Janey wondered if it was the case with this strange note, too. Almost an hour later, she had made no progress in cracking the code and her head was growing heavy with exhaustion.

Janey blew out her candle in defeat and tucked the slip of paper out of sight under her pillow. She settled in beside her mother's warm body, holding Erna Keen tightly to her chest. As she fell asleep, letters and symbols swam before her eyes, swirling up, up, up into the dark sky.

Janey jerked awake in the bright sunlight. She had slept so long and so deeply that it was already mid-morning, and her mother had left for Covent Garden without waking her.

The paper! She dove under the bedding and came up with the little scrap that was her only real clue so far.

As if her mind had been working on the case while she slept, Janey had woken with a new idea. She would take the note to Mr. Denisov, an elderly man who had a small second-hand book cart on Hunton Road. He sold and traded cheap publications to the working men who were lucky enough to have spare time and spare money to spend on reading, and sometimes to lucky street children who happened to have a spare coin in their pocket. Janey had met him years before while she'd still been in school. Mr. Denisov kept an eye out for the serials she favoured - the "penny dreadfuls" that told stories of adventure and crime. He sold them to her for a fair price whenever Janey could afford them. He was the most learned person she knew. Surely, he could crack the code!

She dressed hurriedly and was out the door less than five minutes later.

First, Janey walked up to Mile End Road to check in with Emily, who sleepily told her there'd been nothing of much significance to report – just a light in the attic window at several intervals throughout the night. "I think it was just a single candle", the older girl said, "it moved around periodically, as if someone were reading and shifting their position from time to time."

Janey thought about it. She'd been doing the exact same thing last night. It made a chill run up her spine.

She thanked Emily and promised to meet her again in Selby Passage at dusk. Emily nodded.

"One or two more nights, Janey – that's all I can promise. I'll be too tired to be much use to anyone at all after that!" With a yawn, the girl turned back to the kitchen door, a long and hard day of work ahead of her.

Now Janey hurried down the street to her next destination. As she arrived, Mr. Denisov was just finishing with another customer, pulling a dusty old volume of Charles Dicken's famous novel *Oliver Twist* from the top shelf, where it nestled precariously when the cart was in transit. He greeted her with a nod as he accepted the customer's payment.

"Miss Wiggins!" he said, turning to her. "It's been a long while since your last visit. Don't tell me you've given up on your silly adventure stories? I've got some good ones tucked away for you."

Janey shrugged. She didn't really want to talk about why she'd stayed away for so long. "What have you got?" she asked half-heartedly.

"Treasures!" Mr. Denisov said, pulling out a stack of cheap penny dreadfuls. "*Dan the Detective*?" he asked hopefully. "*Ashton Kirk: Investigator*? How about *Billy Walker: Boy Sleuth*? Or here, there's a new Jim Dale story! *Jim Dale and the Phantom Clue*!"

Janey shook her head. "Do you have any girls' stories?"

Mr. Denisov rifled through his stack. "Well, there's the *Girl's Own Paper*, of course."

Janey wrinkled her nose. "Dull," she said.

"Not much else to tempt you, I'm afraid. I've got *Memoirs of a London Doll* and *The Happy Princess*."

Janey rolled her eyes, and Mr. Denisov chuckled. "That's what I thought. How about *What Katy Did* or *The Governess*? They're both considered very fine and fitting stories for young girls."

"Any adventure in them?"

Denisov pursed his lips. "None that would please a picky child like you. But look, here's the latest edition of *Ernest Keen: Boy Detective*."

Janey took it in her hands, but she felt strangely uninterested. Somehow, Ernest Keen didn't seem quite as exciting as he once had. "I can't afford it. Anything cheaper?"

"Not today, but if you come back next week, there may be something."

Janey nodded. At last, she got down to business. "Have you read any books on codes and ciphers?" she asked him casually, trying to appear idly curious. She knew Mr. Denisov read every book in his cart.

"Codes and..." He trailed off in astonishment. "I can't rightly say that I have. Not much call for the topic around these parts, young lady."

"Oh." Janey's shoulders sagged. She had so hoped that he would be able to help her.

"What are you wanting to know, exactly?" he asked. He knew Janey to be an unusual sort of girl, and liked her for it, but this was an unexpected request even for her.

"Well..." Janey looked at him, considering. Should she trust him? Perhaps his help would be worth the small risk. She slipped the paper out of her pocket and held it up for Mr. Denisov to see.

"I need to crack this code," she explained in a low voice. "I can't tell you why – it's a secret. But it's very important."

Mr. Denisov took the paper from between her fingers and peered at it through his thick spectacles. "Let's see now," he said.

His brow furrowed for an instant and Janey's heart sank. But then the man began laughing. He laughed and laughed and laughed until tears ran down his face. Janey was mystified. She watched him with impatience that quickly turned to embarrassment. Was he laughing at *her*?

Finally, his great bellows of laughter slowed to heaving chuckles, then quieter giggles. Mr. Denisov straightened up, wiping his eyes.

"Oh, Miss Wiggins," he said weakly, "I have uncovered the key to your important secret code – it's cabbages!"

His laughter threatened to erupt all over again, but Janey cut him off, her face flaming. "Cabbages? What do you *mean*, cabbages?"

"My dear girl. Where did you find this?"

"I told you! It's a secret! It's a very important professional secret. I will not reveal it! And I'm not your girl!" Janey stomped her foot for good measure. She didn't know whether she was more angry, embarrassed or hurt, but she did know that she was beginning to feel a horrible crushing sensation in her chest.

Mr. Denisov laughed again, but not quite as much. Perhaps he noticed her distress, and he was not a cruel man.

"It is not a secret code, child," he said at last. "It's Cyrillic script – a language. Used by millions of people around the world, and a goodly number of them are in London. More and more every day, fleeing dangerous places like Russia, my own motherland."

Janey's every instinct was to run from this humiliating scene, but she forced herself to swallow her pride. Nothing was more important than getting the facts.

She thought for a moment.

"Why are they fleeing Russia? It's very far to come!"

Mr. Densiov nodded. "That's true enough, but Janey, many of our neighbours here are from foreign lands, and there are many different reasons for them to come. I myself came to London from Moscow as a young man, looking for work. Not everyone has the same life as you," he reproved her gently.

"So, they come for work?" she asked. That made sense. Everyone needed money to buy their bread.

"Not always. Sometimes they seek refuge from war or other horrors. Sometimes they seek the freedom to practice their own religions. In Russia, we Jews are treated very poorly. We are harassed to such a degree that many of us choose to flee. Many have ended up here – and more arrive every day.

In fact, they've just opened a new East End Synagogue to accommodate the numbers! Yes, even the East End, with its pickpockets and cutthroats and thieves, can sometimes be preferable to the terrible injustices that take place in the world."

"Does-" Janey hesitated. "Does this paper talk about that?"

The man snorted. "It's a shopping list, child. Cabbages, bread, butter, milk – quite a lot of milk, cheese, three sausages, three pies, three kippers... Shall I go on? Someone didn't want her husband to forget the essentials."

Janey's shoulders slumped. The crushing feeling in her chest was back. A shopping list? That was useless – worse than useless! She'd let her childish fancies get in the way of a simple truth.

She grabbed the paper back from Mr. Denisov and slipped away into the passing crowd, muttering her thanks. She heard him call after her in a mystified kind of voice, but Janey didn't look back. She didn't know if she'd ever be able to face him again.

A secret code! How stupid must he think her!

Holmes's voice echoed in her head, "Detectives trade in facts. The simplest explanation is usually the correct one – no matter how much we want the fantastic to be real."

If that's what detectives do, Janey thought, *then I am certainly not one.*

Chapter Seventeen

As if by habit, Janey's feet turned to Pearl Street.

She sat in the entrance to Selby Passage for the day, hiding herself well under her shawl as she'd done the day before. The difference in how she felt left her head almost spinning. Instead of the thrill and excitement of the day before, Janey was dejected. She watched the house closely, but only because of her promise to Holmes. She had no expectations that a stupid poor street girl like her could solve anything.

Under her gaze, the house's inhabitants seemed to go about their everyday lives. Janey saw the woman at the window a few times, but she was doing nothing more exciting than opening the curtain to let in the morning sun, or walking past on her way to some other part of the house. The man stepped out of the front door once to smoke his pipe in the fresh morning air, but that was all. *It's nothing*, Janey thought to herself. *This is meaningless. I have nothing to report.*

In the late afternoon, a light snow began to fall. It wasn't enough to stick, but just enough to dampen Janey's clothing and leave her teeth chattering. Nearly numb with cold, she thought she'd never been so miserable. There was nothing to do except sit and freeze and think about how useless and stupid she was. At least the Vigilance Committee was nowhere to be seen. Janey felt grateful for small mercies.

Rose didn't show up after school. Janey didn't blame her. The girl probably had better things to do – things that included warm fires, blankets and dinner.

Janey's stomach growled. She would eat later that night with her mother. Until then, she would have to be patient.

As the sun slowly went down and the city lost the light, the temperature dropped even lower. By the time Emily arrived to take her night watch, Janey could barely speak - she was shivering so hard. She knew she'd have to get indoors soon, or risk illness.

When she finally saw Emily round the corner of the passage, Janey was in such low spirits that she burst into tears.

"Now, now!" Emily said in surprise. "I'm not *that* terrible to look at, am I?"

Janey sniffed miserably, but she couldn't help but smile a little. Emily was the kindest soul on earth, her warm, eager eyes were all the more beautiful in their familiarity. Emily was her only cousin, and Janey couldn't deny that it was comforting to have an older girl in her corner sometimes. She could always count on Emily.

The older girl crouched down beside her, looking concerned. "Have you eaten?" she asked.

Janey shook her head.

"Well there you are, then," Emily said kindly. "No one can be happy on an empty stomach. Here." She pulled something wrapped in a handkerchief out of her pocket and handed it to Janey. The little bundle was deliciously warm. She unwrapped it with trembling fingers to find a heaped, steaming pile of roasted chestnuts, fragrant and meaty. She leaned down to breathe in the steam.

"Go on," Emily said. "They're for us. A treat to start the night."

Janey felt the warmth of the packet start to seep into her fingers. She picked out a chestnut and peeled off the charred shell that clung to it.

"Thank you," she said as she popped it into her mouth. "I don't deserve a treat, though."

Emily snorted. "Didn't stop you from taking one, though, did it?" she teased.

Janey blushed. "Hush, you."

They ate in silence for several minutes.

When all the chestnuts were gone, Janey broke the silence. "You were right, Emily, about the note we found yesterday. It wasn't a secret code. It was a shopping list written in Russian. It was *nothing*, and I was too stupid to see it. I have no business pretending to be a detective. I'm just a stupid girl."

She felt her eyes begin to prickle with tears, but quickly blinked them back.

Emily shrugged her shoulders. "Good. You found out the language, and you found out what the writing meant. That's not nothing, Janey. Not to my way of thinking. You're ahead of where you were."

Janey said nothing. Maybe it was the food warming her stomach, or the kindly company, but she began to wonder if she'd been too harsh on herself.

"What is that Mr. Holmes told you?" Emily asked. "The first principle of detection?"

"Start with the facts," Janey answered quietly.

"Right. You have those now. You're doing well."

Janey frowned. Could Emily be right?

Suddenly, she sat up straighter. What had been on the list, again? What had Mr. Denisov said?

"Observe the details…" she whispered, thinking furiously. "Cabbages!" she exclaimed at last. "Cabbages, bread, butter, cheese… A lot of milk! Three sausages, three pies, three kippers."

Emily looked at her in confusion.

"Emily!" Janey asked urgently, "how many people have you ever seen in the house?"

"Just the two, the man and woman."

"No sign of anyone else?"

"Never."

"Right!" Janey exclaimed. "So why are they shopping for three? And why do they need so much milk? Emily!" She looked at her cousin with wide eyes. "Where is the child they're feeding?"

Emily let out a low whistle. "Where indeed?" she asked.

Involuntarily, they both looked up at the attic window.

"Can you stay tonight?" Janey asked.

"Of course. I can stay all night, and I'll try my best to keep awake."

Janey nodded. She knew they couldn't keep this up forever. "Well, do what you can. I'll see you in the morning. And Emily?" Her cousin looked up at her as she rose to leave. "Thank you."

Emily smiled and nodded. "Any time, Janey. Any time."

Chapter Eighteen

Janey arrived home a full hour before her mother. She would be hurrying home on her long walk now, dodging the icy puddles of sleet hidden by a thin layer of snow.

Janey pulled off her wet things and set them over a chair to dry. With shaking fingers, she lit a fire in the grate. She pulled the blanket off the bed and wrapped it around her, edging as near to the small fire as she dared. It would not do to singe their one good blanket.

It took almost half an hour for the shivering to subside.

She was almost dozing – finally warm by the fire, sitting with Erna Keen in her lap and playing idly with her yarn hair, listening lazily for her mother's foot on the stair – when she sat up abruptly. There was the sound of a tread on the stair that she didn't recognize; a loud, sturdy step climbing rapidly.

A knock came at the door. Janey blinked in astonishment. No one ever visited her here, except perhaps Rose, but that had not been a child's step.

Cautiously, she edged towards the door, trying not to make a sound. Her mother had always warned never to open the door to people she didn't recognize.

"Miss Wiggins?" a voice called. "Miss Jane Wiggins?"

"Yes?" Janey replied, too astonished to hold back anymore.

"Delivery for you, Miss."

Janey's mouth fell open in shock. She'd never received a delivery before in her life!

She threw open the door. An officially-dressed delivery boy was standing in the dingy hall with a package in his hands. He passed it over, nodded smartly, and turned on his heel and was gone.

Janey closed the door behind him and returned to her place by the fire. She lit a candle with hands that were trembling – with excitement rather than cold.

The package was fair sized, too big to hold in a single hand, and heavy. It was wrapped in brown paper, with her name and address printed clearly on the front. She carefully pulled open the paper, taking care not to rip it and looked at the contents in astonishment - three beautiful books, all brand new, and a small notebook and pencil set. The same, she noticed, as the notebook Dr. Watson had been using that night in the tea shop.

Janey searched through the discarded paper wrapping and the pages of the books, looking for a letter or card to explain it all, but there was nothing. She was about to give up when a thought struck her. She turned to the first page of the notebook, and indeed, it was filled with the same tiny, careful script she had seen in Dr. Watson's own notebook.

"*Dear Miss Wiggins,*" the letter began,

I hope this note finds you well, and that you will excuse the liberty I am taking in sending it to you. It occurred to Mr. Holmes and I, after we parted, that you would benefit from some materials to help you in your new Irregular position. Please use this notebook to carefully document any observations you may find relevant. Holmes asks me to remind you that careful and precise recording of facts is vital to the practice of detection.

I have also included several books for your continuing education and also, I must confess, for your amusement. Holmes has not yet written his long-planned book on the practice of detection, but he recommends this book by the French thief-turned-policeman Monsieur Vidocq as being very helpful to aspiring detectives. As it is drawn from real life, it is far more useful than any penny dreadful fiction. It is a memoir of his very interesting life - The True Remembrances of Vidocq.

Second, I have included a volume recounting Holmes's own cases, which I have written up as short stories that have become quite popular. Here are The Adventures of Sherlock Holmes. *Holmes wishes the stories to be informative, and I wish them to be entertaining. Perhaps you will find them to be both. And finally, I have obtained the schoolbook used in the class above yours at the East End Charity School. Forgive me, but I suspect you will relish the opportunity to keep up with your studies, even in so informal a manner.*

Please remember, above all else, that you must come to Baker Street if your situation appears to be at all dangerous. We would never wish to endanger you – for you are, after all, our agent and our responsibility.

Your friend,

Dr. John Watson

Janey hugged the books tight to her chest for several minutes. When at last she heard her mother's tired foot on the step, she carefully slipped them under the mattress, right where she slept, propping Erna Keen carefully beside them so that no gap would be visible. She would be able to feel their bulky shape pressing through the mattress all night – a reminder that they were hers. Three new books, all to herself! She'd never owned anything so precious, but more precious still was the message they conveyed - that Holmes and Watson believed in her.

Chapter Nineteen

Janey jerked awake. Her back was sore where it had been pressed into cold brick all day, and her legs ached under her. She'd been sitting in Selby Passage, watching the uneventful household movements within 54 Pearl Street. Rose had joined her for a few hours after school, and then gone home to her brother. Emily was taking a night to rest up – properly – in her own bed.

She deserves a nice long break, the girl thought.

Janey planned to sit in the passage until just before midnight, and then run home to her mother – dodging the Vigilance gang that would surely be patrolling by then.

It had grown dark while Janey slept, and she cursed herself for her lack of attention. She couldn't allow her attention to flag. She shook her head to clear the last tendrils of sleep from her mind. What if something important had happened?

Janey didn't know how much time had passed, but it must be approaching midnight, she thought. She should probably head home.

She looked across to the house and surveyed each window. All was dark and quiet. But still, Janey had a nagging feeling that something was wrong.

Suddenly, there was movement by the side of the house. Someone – several someones, in fact – were creeping around to the front, staying low and carefully keeping to the shadows. They were almost entirely invisible in the darkness; it must have been their whispers or a foot scuffing against a cobblestone that had pulled her from her dreams.

Janey strained her eyes, trying to see what they were doing. There seemed to be three or four of them, all huddled together at the front of the house. She couldn't make out their features, nor hear the words they spoke to each other as they stood at the front of the house.

Her heart began to pound. Were they thieves? *Murderers*? Would they break into the house and rouse the occupants? What could there be inside worth stealing? This was a poor neighbourhood, Janey couldn't imagine anyone would bother with it. But what were they *doing*?

She edged forward slowly, working her way to the very opening of Selby Passage, trying to get as close as she could without being noticed.

There was a sound - the clink of metal against stone as one of the men put something down on the ground. Someone angrily shushed him. Janey crept closer still until she was in Pearl Street itself, crouched in the shadows, when she finally made out a few words.

"Where shall we do it?"

"Here. The wall by the window."

"Aye. Everyone will see."

"Did you bring the brush?"

"Of course I brought the brush! What do you take me for?"

"Here, give it to me. I'll do it. I don't trust your spelling."

And then there was silence again, the men bent to their mysterious task.

"There," one whispered at last. "All done."

"Serves 'em right," another said, and spat on the ground.

"Come on. Let's go."

The men disappeared back into the shadows, leaving the street silent and deserted. Janey had been listening so hard she didn't realize she'd stopped breathing. She forced herself to relax, taking several deep breaths. Whatever the danger had been, it was now gone.

Clock bells rang out abruptly, their peals tolling the hour. Janey jumped, then started to count. 9, 10, 11... It was midnight! Her mother would be furious with her for missing curfew again.

But before Janey could head home, she had one last task to accomplish. She darted across Pearl Street to the place the men had been moments before. Carefully, she lit a match and looked around, crouching to examine the ground for any clues the men might have left behind. There was nothing. She blew out her match and slumped against the wall in disappointment, but pulled herself quickly upright again when she felt a wet, sticky substance on the surface of the bricks behind her.

Quickly, she lit another match. There, written in big,

black painted letters was the terrible slogan:

ENGLAND FOR THE ENGLISH

FOREIGNERS GO HOME!

Chapter Twenty

Janey barely slept that night. In addition to the scolding she'd received from her mother, the events of the evening in Pearl Street kept playing through her head, over and over. Again she heard the men's ugly whispers as they worked, saw their silhouettes in the shadows. She shivered and rolled closer to her sleeping mother, pulling Erna Keen to her chest and sandwiching herself between them.

Sometimes, it felt like her mind was a dangerous place to be. Her imagination was too real, too frightening. Janey couldn't always control it. Staring out into the darkness of her room, the dank and filth of Selby Passage haunted her senses. In the strange state between sleep and wakefulness, she could almost believe she was back there again. Every creak of the old, wooden house, every crackle of the dying fire in the hearth seemed strange and ominous. Behind her closed eyes, all she saw was the Pearl Street Ghost's blank stare, boring into her, swooping down from its perch at the window to wreak terrible vengeance upon the men who had defaced its home. A ghostly howl of rage filled her ears.

She shook her head frantically and jerked fully awake, burrowing deeper into her pillow. Beside her, her mother slept peacefully. Janey envied her, and tried to match her own quick breath to the older woman's slow breathing.

She was safe, she reminded herself. There was no such thing as ghosts.

Eventually, Janey dropped off into a fitful sleep again.

She woke early, though – even before her mother did. Shivering, she leapt out of bed and dressed in the cold, without making a fire. She'd warm herself by running all the way back to Pearl Street. She wanted to be there when the sun rose.

Janey knelt by the bed to kiss her mother's cheek. "Have a good day, mother. I'm off to Mrs. Eastley's. She asked me to watch the baby this morning." She winced at the small lie, but knew her mother would not approve of her real purpose this morning.

Her mother murmured something back, but Janey was already out the door.

By the time she arrived at 54 Pearl Street and took her accustomed place in Selby Passage, Janey was warm already, her cheeks pink with exercise.

The black lettering defacing the front of the house was an ugly thing to see; a wound slashed into a home she'd become to think of as kind and friendly, familiar. Janey hated it with every fibre of her being.

She sat and watched as the sun came up. The street awoke. Dock hands and labourers started making their way through, some with their tired eyes trained on the ground before them, but others noticed the lettering. Of those that noticed, most made no sign. Perhaps a dozen grimaced. Two or three threw garbage at the house - the core of an apple; a scrap of bread. One threw his lit cigarette at the door. It rolled away, sputtered and went out, to Janey's relief.

After an hour or so, the woman of the house opened the door and came out to the step to shake out the tablecloth.

Janey was watching closely when she finally noticed the dark letters. She gasped in horror, her face draining of all colour. She all but ran back into the house, slamming the door shut behind her.

A few minutes later, the man opened the door and looked out apprehensively. There was no one passing by just then, so he opened the door wider and stepped out. In his hands were a steaming bucket of water and a stiff brush.

He set them down in front of the wall and carefully rolled up his sleeves. Then he took up the brush, dipped it in the water, and set to work cleaning the terrible words. It was slow, heavy work - the paint was stubborn, and it took many long minutes for his work to show any effect at all. But slowly, the letters faded under the brush.

As he worked and the morning wore on, foot traffic on Pearl Street increased. Many men and several women passed by. None spoke a word to him. Janey noticed that although no one had the nerve to insult him to his face, neither did anyone offer to help him – not even the neighbours or shop keepers nearby.

Janey noticed the front window curtains twitch open several times. The woman was keeping a close eye on the proceedings, she suspected.

Suddenly, there was a burst of noise down the street. Three men were swaggering down Pearl Street, talking loudly and laughing uproariously at their own jokes. With a start, Janey recognized one of them as Mr. Crawford. At the sight of him, Janey squeezed her hands into fists, nails digging painfully into her palms.

The men approached 54 Pearl Street with looks of barely-disguised glee. They stopped to watch the man clean. Janey saw the man's back stiffen with fear, but he did not stop his work.

"Hey!" Mr. Crawford called, at last. "Hey, you! What's going on here?"

The man turned, finally. He put down his brush and looked at the men, saying nothing.

"I asked you a question. What're you doing?"

Again, the man made no answer but simply stood, looking steadily at the men.

"Do you understand me? Are you too stupid to speak? Or are you just rude?" Mr. Crawford's voice was menacing, and he took a step closer to the man. "I know you can't read, so I stopped by to make sure you understood the message we left for you last night," he said, gesturing to the painted letters. Suddenly he lunged forward, grabbing the man by the collar of his shirt and shaking him, hard. "We don't want your kind here, bringing your filth and your crime to our city. *Get out if you know what's good for you*," Crawford hissed.

Then he thrust the man back against the wall and turned away, sauntering down the street with his two laughing cronies in tow. Over his shoulder, Mr. Crawford called out one last insult as he went, "Nothing but foreign trash."

The man stayed where he had fallen against the wall until Crawford and his men were out of sight. He shakily pulled himself up and returned to his work. He did not stop until the last bit of lettering had disappeared and the bricks at the front of his house were cleaner than they ever had been.

Janey felt a little shaky herself. If this family had indeed fled Russia for a better life, it was hard to believe London could be much of an improvement.

Chapter Twenty-One

Several days passed uneventfully. Janey, Rose, and Emily took their turns at watch, but there were no more run-ins with the Vigilance Committee.

Janey quickly became familiar with the daily routine of 54 Pearl Street's residents. The woman came out mid-morning to shake out a carpet and broom. She answered the door when peddlers came to sell their wares, and always bought something from the people who stopped, although she was careful not to tarry in the street. Mid-afternoon, the man stepped out and lit his pipe.

Janey was beginning to notice how people lived their days according to regular rhythms. She pulled out her new notebook and entered in the household's daily routine as she had observed it.

The man finished his pipe. Instead of going back inside, though, as he usually did, on this particular day – three days after the vandalism – he opened the door and called in.

The woman joined him on the step, dressed smartly but sensibly in a warm wool coat and hat.

The man offered her his arm, which she took, and together they looked nervously up and down the street. He drew a key from his pocket and carefully locked the door, testing it several times to make sure it was properly fastened.

Then the couple turned down the lane.

Janey was surprised. This was the first time they'd ever

gone out together – the first time the house had been left empty. She stood up and followed them at a discrete distance. They walked on, not turning or stopping, until they reached Commercial Street. There they turned left and walked several blocks up to the new East London Synagogue, where they disappeared into the thronging crowd. Janey turned back, considering. Since they'd gone into the synagogue, Janey reasoned that they'd be away from their home for at least an hour.

An idea struck her. She knew it was a bad one and Dr. Watson would not approve.

But she also had a very strong suspicion that Mr. Holmes himself would encourage her. Detectives had to take risks sometimes, didn't they?

Janey had, by now, arrived back at the house. She looked up and down Pearl Street. There was no one in sight.

Trying to look casual, she strolled across the lane and stood with her back to the house's front window. Casually, she reached behind her and tried to push it open. It wouldn't budge. She tried again, but it was stuck tight.

Janey ducked quickly around to the side. Between the house and the building next to it, there was a gap barely big enough for one of the neighbourhood stray cats to fit through. She peeked in and saw a window ledge jutting out from the side, about halfway down the side of the house. A window looking out onto a brick wall? Surely they would not have been so careful about locking that one!

Janey thought she could just fit into the gap if she

squeezed herself very tightly. She removed her bulky shawl and tucked it on the ground so that it would look like nothing more than a pile of old rags. Then she squeezed herself into the gap.

It was so narrow that she had to walk sideways, shuffling along instead of taking full steps. She inched her way painfully along. Her face was pressed against the brick, and every step she took caused her to scrape up against it. Inch by inch she went until, reaching forward, she felt the edge of the window ledge with the very tips of her fingers.

Janey edged closer. Soon, she was standing right in front of the window, peering in. She was looking into a shabby sitting room, furnished with a dinner table and two wooden chairs, and two old armchairs grouped around the fire. The fire in the hearth was banked, awaiting the couple's return.

Carefully, she grasped the window frame and pulled it gently upwards.

The window slid open with ease.

Heart hammering in her chest, Janey slid the window all the way up in the frame. She scrambled up over the sill, pulling in her skirts and shutting the window behind her.

She was in!

Janey took a deep breath.

She was standing alone in the ghost house.

Chapter Twenty-Two

Janey looked around her slowly, fighting a feeling of unreality. She could hardly believe she'd done it! It took a moment for her to gather her wits. She didn't know how much time was left; she should make a quick search of the house and learn everything she could about the inhabitants, then depart as quickly as possible.

The first thing to do was to look over the main floor. The house was small and cramped. There was a dining table under the front window, and a couple of armchairs grouped around the fireplace, but little room for anything else. Towards the rear of the house was a single bedroom not much larger than Janey's. Across from it was a steep flight of stairs ascended to the attic. The tiny kitchen, barely large enough to be called one, in truth, was tucked away under the attic stairs.

The most astonishing thing, however, was the huge bookcase that stood proudly beside the fireplace. Every shelf – from floor to ceiling, and stretching almost as wide as the wall itself – was stuffed full with dozens and dozens of books. Maybe hundreds! Janey had never seen so many all in one place. There were more books than Mr Denisov had in his cart. Far more, even, than the charity school had had. Janey breathed in deeply and felt as if she could even smell them - dry paper, dust, and ink.

What kind of people could have a need for so many books? Who could possibly afford so many?

She walked over to a shelf and pulled a book down

randomly. It fell open in her hands, the script was what she had come to know as Cyrillic. She carefully placed it back and scanned the shelf. All of the books seemed to be in that same language. But the next shelf down, she noted, was German – a language Janey recognized from a few lessons on European languages she'd taken during her school days. She looked more closely at the spines of the other books around the room. There must have been at least five or six languages included! Who could read so many? Of the English titles mixed in amongst the rest, she found works on science, history, mathematics, art, and dozens of novels.

Janey ran her hands over the spines, trying to memorize the feel of the gilt lettering, the good leather, the rich fabrics that bound them.

A particularly vibrant blue book caught her eye. She picked it up carefully. "The Moonstone" was written in gold lettering across the spine, by Wilkie Collins. Full of curiosity, she opened the book to the first page, and was immediately drawn into a tale of cursed diamonds and adventure on the Indian subcontinent. What an extraordinary book!

Janey was just beginning to lose herself in the story when she suddenly remembered herself. She was running short on time! The man and woman could be back any second. Regretfully, she replaced the book on the shelf. Page 21, she told herself. She didn't know why, but it seemed worth remembering.

With a sigh, she returned to the business of detecting.

Glancing across the room, Janey saw a framed portrait

of the couple on the wall. They were younger, and seemed somehow happier in the portrait than they did now. The woman's smile was warm and untinged with sadness while the man's eyes had none of the nervous wariness they now held.

She turned to survey the table. A teapot sat in the middle. When Janey put a hand to it, it was still a little warm. Beyond it, she saw something glittering in the dim light. She reached out, careful not to disturb the stacks of books and papers that lay on the table.

It was a silver locket. The oval pendant had a beautiful floral pattern etched into the front. The chain was heavy and sturdy, as if the owner didn't want to risk losing it. Carefully, Janey wedged her thumbnail into the catch and the locket clicked open. Inside was a portrait of a boy. She drew closer to the window to catch the light in order to examine the photograph more closely.

The boy was beautiful. He was just a little older than Rose. He had bright, serious eyes that stared straight at the camera, his mouth carried a hint of the same warm smile Janey had seen on the woman in the photo. His dark blond hair was trimmed neatly across his forehead, and he was dressed in clothing that looked strange to Janey - old fashioned, slightly different than anything she'd seen before.

She stared at the photo for a long time. "Who are you?" she whispered. "And *where* are you?"

Suddenly, she felt ashamed of herself for invading this family's home by entering it uninvited. She had a strong suspicion that she would like them very much if she ever had a chance to properly meet them.

Janey closed the locket and replaced it carefully on the table. Too much time had passed – she would have to finish her search quickly.

She went to examine the small bedroom at the back of the house, and found it to be entirely ordinary. There was a bed made up with cotton sheets, a wardrobe, a single chair, a washstand, and nothing else.

Across from the bedroom door were the steps up to the attic. She had saved them for last.

Silently, she climbed the steep and narrow staircase. At the top stood a plain wood door. She grasped the doorknob and, heart in her throat, turned it.

It didn't move.

She tried again, pulling harder this time. Still the door didn't budge.

From behind the door came a sudden crash, and her blood froze in her veins. Next came the sound of feet skittering across the attic floor. It wasn't the sound of mice – Janey knew that sound well enough – but the definite sound of human footfalls. Then, the house returned to silence.

There was someone in there! But who? Why? For a ghost, the footsteps sounded awfully real, thumping around like that.

Janey laughed at herself. It was not a ghost. It couldn't be!

She was just about to call out, to make contact with the mysterious person in the attic when she heard something even more frightening - the sound of a key scraping at the front door.

In a heartbeat, Janey was down the steps and across to the side window, yanking it open and diving through. She pulled it shut behind her just as the front door opened.

Janey was panting, but safe once more in the cramped space between the buildings. She'd made it! Her heart hammered in her chest. That had been a close call.

Chapter Twenty-Three

Janey picked up her shawl from the ground and hurried down Pearl Street, wrapping it around her as she went. She made an important decision. There was finally enough information to warrant a report to Mr. Holmes and Dr. Watson. She had seen the ghost-like creature with her own eyes. She had learned about the household's routine. She had been inside the house itself and observed all the details she could. She had even heard someone moving about in the attic!

Yes, she thought, *it's definitely time to pay Holmes and Watson a visit.*

Janey rarely left her neighbourhood in the East End, but she knew the quickest ways to get to most places in central London. It would take her close to two hours to make the walk to Baker Street, but she didn't mind at all. It would give her time to organize her thoughts and decide exactly what to tell her employers – and how.

She walked quickly through the busy streets, dodging peddlers and children and pigeons as she went, hoping to get there and back home long before her mother would miss her. As she walked, Janey heard the chimes of a church clock strike 4 o'clock. She quickened her pace.

By the time she arrived at Baker Street, her face was pink from the exercise and her nose dripped in the cold wind. Hurriedly, she wiped it in her handkerchief, stuffing it back into her sleeve afterward. She straightened her shawl and tried to smooth her uncooperative hair down with her hand.

221 Baker Street was a nondescript block of flats. Janey felt somehow disappointed – she had imagined her wealthy employers to be living in the lap of luxury, not in this plain brick building without any markings indicating the presence of the two remarkable men.

Janey stood in front of the building for several minutes, mustering up the courage to knock. She'd never paid a visit like this before. Butterflies fluttered nervously in her stomach, but she forced herself to walk up the three steps to the plain, brown door and knock.

An elderly woman answered the door. She looked down at Janey with disapproving eyes. "Yes?" she asked. "I suppose you'll be wanting Mr. Holmes?"

Janey nodded mutely.

The woman sighed. "Follow me," she said. "But be sure to wipe your shoes on the mat! I've just washed the floors."

Janey followed the woman up a narrow flight of stairs, making certain not to leave a single drip behind her. The woman stopped on the landing at a door marked "B" and knocked gently.

"Mr. Holmes?" she called. "You have a—" she hesitated, looking at Janey's ragged shawl and unkempt appearance – "a young visitor."

"Do I indeed?" exclaimed a voice from within. "By all means, Mrs. Hudson, please show her in."

"And bring tea and sandwiches, if you would be so

kind," a second voice added.

Mrs. Hudson looked at Janey more kindly than she had. "In you go," she said. "I'll be back shortly with your tea." With that, she pushed Janey into the room and shut the door behind her.

"Miss Wiggins!" Holmes exclaimed, rising from his corner desk. "I trust you have information for us?"

"Holmes, please!" Dr. Watson scolded. "First things first!" He rose from the divan to shake her hand. Holmes just grimaced and returned to his desk. "Are you well?"

"Yes, sir," Janey answered, feeling almost as if she should curtsey. When she had first met Holmes and Watson, they had been on her territory. It had not occurred to her to be intimidated by them. But standing in their fine, warm sitting room, surrounded by good furniture and excellent carpets, she was fairly overwhelmed.

As she always did, Janey hid her uncertainty under a veil of false confidence.

"I'm very well, thank you," she continued. "And yes, I do have information for you."

Dr. Watson's eyes sparkled. "Please, sit down and tell us all about it."

He guided Janey over to a comfortable armchair set near to the fire. He returned to his divan and discretely removed a notebook and pencil from his pocket. Janey pulled her own matching notebook out of a fold in her shawl. She glanced uncertainly at Mr. Holmes, who had not looked up from his reading. But Dr. Watson smiled encouragingly at her, so she opened her notebook and began to speak.

She explained clearly and precisely everything she had said and done since she had begun watching the house. Although Holmes continued to stare down at his newspaper, once or twice he interrupted in order to ask for clarification on some small point of fact. Each time, Janey had an answer at the ready. He nodded tightly to himself and allowed her to carry on.

Watson, she was gratified to notice, was scribbling down details in his own notebook.

Once she began describing the events of her afternoon – secretly entering the ghost house and conducting her search – she had Holmes's full attention. He swivelled in his seat to watch Janey as she spoke. After a moment, he stood and paced back and forth across the room as she spoke. Dr. Watson, however, narrowed his lips in disapproval. She had not followed his rule about limiting her role to observing only, but she could not be sorry for that now.

Finally came the end of her tale - the sounds from the attic, the couple's unexpected return, and Janey's own narrow escape.

Holmes raised his eyebrows at that. "Are you quite certain they did not see you?" he demanded.

Janey nodded. "They did not. It all came off perfectly."

"Good lord!" Watson interjected. "What a risk you took! What if they had found you – a stranger – inside their house?"

Janey shrugged. "They didn't, did they?"

Dr. Watson looked flabbergasted for a moment, and then broke out into a long peal of laughter. "Good lord," he said again. "You and Holmes are two peas in a pod. It's truly extraordinary."

Holmes snorted. "I shall try not to be offended, Watson, that you compare me to a scruffy, uneducated street girl."

Janey glared at him. "And *I* shall try not to be offended, Dr. Watson, that you compare *me* to a rude arrogant grown-up who believes he is better than everyone else!" she exclaimed.

"Heaven help me," Watson sighed, looking between them. "Janey, you have done excellent work for us, and we thank you. Here is your pay." He handed her a coin, which she clutched tightly in her fist. "However," he continued, "you must take more care in the future. Never endanger yourself on our behalf. Do you promise?"

Janey nodded solemnly. "But sir, I was in no danger. Even if the couple had found me in their home, I do not believe they would have hurt me. They only ever act with kindness! I have never seen anything but goodness in either one of them."

Holmes sighed. "Looks can be deceiving, child."

Janey snapped her mouth shut. She didn't feel like explaining to Holmes that she'd been watching these people for days – that she knew their routines and observed their interactions and had been in their home, that she knew them far better than he seemed to think her capable of. He was a detective. He should understand that she was just trying to learn to be one too. If he didn't – well, that was his problem.

Janey stood up. "What are you going to do now?" she asked.

Holmes hesitated, glancing at Watson for a long moment before speaking. "We're going to act," he said at last. "We must."

"What is your theory of the case?" she asked.

"My theory is none of your concern," Holmes said under his breath, pacing back and forth wildly across the room.

"Holmes, really!" Watson said crossly. "Miss Wiggins is your agent and your helper!"

But somehow, Janey was less offended by this than she had been just minutes before. Holmes was agitated, thinking hard. She couldn't fault him for forgetting his manners in such a state – it was possible, after all, that there was much at stake.

Holmes stopped short at Watson's reproof. He strode over to Janey and knelt before her.

"Miss Wiggins," he said, "you must excuse me. I am greatly concerned for the welfare of the poor creature locked up in the attic of that house, and all of my attention must be focused on the mystery. It makes it difficult to remember courtesies. It is only natural that you ask me my plans. Hear them, then." His eyes bore into her own with an intensity she had never seen in a human being before, as if his very thoughts had caught fire and were burning dreadfully inside his skull. She wondered if it hurt.

"I greatly fear that the couple you so admire are in fact criminals of the worst sort - kidnappers. They have taken a child – under circumstances that are not yet clear to me – and locked them in their attic. Perhaps they are after money, planning to return the child once its parents pay a certain amount of ransom. Perhaps they have some other motive with which we are not yet familiar. The point is - the child must be saved and returned to its parents, and we must do so before the couple realizes they are being watched."

Janey had been slowly shaking her head throughout Holmes's long speech. She broke in. "No, sir! I do not believe it. There is nothing I have seen that supports your theory!"

"*Everything* you have seen supports my theory," Holmes roared. It seemed that he was out of patience. But so was Janey.

She stamped her foot. "If there truly is a kidnapped child in the attic, why would he not cry out? Or escape through a window?"

Her questions pulled Holmes up short. He blinked at her. "He may have been threatened. He may be too afraid. He could be tied up. There are a dozen possible reasons, at least!"

Janey shook her head. "Those are not the simplest solutions, Mr. Holmes."

Holmes snorted. "You might be an irregular, Miss

Wiggins, but *I'm* the detective. I don't need a child to teach me my business, and I do not have time to explain the case to you further. Goodbye, and thank you for your help. We will contact you again when we next require assistance."

Janey shook her head again, but she could do nothing to change Holmes's mind. "When will you go?" she asked helplessly.

"Tonight. Very late," he replied. "When the household is asleep, we will enter and we will recover the child."

Janey stood without another word and went to the door. There she turned, and Dr. Watson was at her elbow.

"Don't mind Holmes," he said kindly. "He's not a polite man, but he's very good at what he does."

"Yes," Janey said. "I think he probably often is." And then, more shyly, she added, "thank you for the books, sir." She had no idea how to thank him for such a grand and perfect gift, and so she impulsively grabbed him in a quick, heart-felt hug before ducking out into the corridor. Janey was down the stairs and out the front door before Watson could even blink.

Chapter Twenty-Four

Janey ran all the way back to the East End, retracing her earlier steps but moving twice as quickly. She had one thought in her head - that Holmes was wrong, and that she needed to solve the case before he arrived and made a disastrous mistake. She was surprised at how protective she felt of those people; somehow, she *knew* they weren't criminals, and she was desperate now to prove it.

As she turned onto Commercial Street, she saw familiar figures up ahead - Jim Crawford and his father were walking slowly up the street, stopping to chat with shopkeepers as they went. The sun was setting. Janey turned her head and hurried past them, keeping well out of their way, hoping they wouldn't notice her slip onto Pearl Street. Soon they'd begin their nightly patrol. She needed to be in position before then.

When Janey arrived, Rose was sitting in their usual spot. Her eyes were glued to the house as the girl shivered with the cold.

She jumped up when Janey arrived and kissed her on the cheek.

"Janey!" she exclaimed. "I'm so sorry I missed our last watch, but I have wonderful news! Mother is home from the hospital! She came back yesterday. We were so shocked you could have knocked us over with a feather! She's back! She's really, truly back with us! She's terribly thin and weak, but the cough is so much better – it's a miracle! The doctors said she can't infect anyone anymore, so she might as well be resting at home. Oh, Janey, I'm so happy!"

Tears welled in the younger girl's eyes. Her face glowed with joy. Janey pulled her into a hug.

"That *is* wonderful news!" she said, grinning widely. She was intensely relieved. Not many people survived a bout with tuberculosis; she had had grave fears for Rose's mother's life.

"Go home to her," she told Rose. "I'll take over here. Emily will join me shortly, and we'll plan for the night. I'll see you tomorrow." She didn't want to burden Rose with the case at such a happy time, nor did she wish to involve her in anything that could be dangerous.

Rose nodded happily and kissed Janey's cheek.

"Watch yourself, though," Janey cautioned. "The Crawfords are about."

"I will." Rose flashed another radiant smile and then turned and disappeared down Pearl Street.

Janey smiled fondly after her for a moment, before her thoughts returned to the case at hand. She glanced at the house. A warm glow filled the curtained front window; the evening lamp had been lit. Gratefully, she realized she had an hour or two to think before the couple went to bed.

She sank down into her usual spot in Selby Passage, staring hard. She had to find out who, or what, was in the attic and she had to do it before Holmes and Watson arrived. But how could she get in?

Suddenly, Janey jumped up. The small house was wedged in between two larger buildings – she had never once thought to look around the back! The girl could have laughed at her own foolishness if she hadn't been so cross with herself. Why, examining the house from every angle should have been the very first thing she did!

Janey raced around the strip of buildings into the narrow alley that ran behind them. Gazing up, she realized that she was very, very lucky indeed. The attic of 54 Pearl Street had a second window facing the back alley. Even better, the taller neighbouring building had steps up to its second storey that would give her access to the roof of number 54! Janey sighed with relief. She had a plan. She only had to wait until the house was sleeping to put it into action.

Chapter Twenty-Five

Night fell. Janey waited impatiently in Selby Passage for the inhabitants of 54 Pearl Street to extinguish their lights and go to sleep. Emily arrived when the clocks rang out at 9 o'clock, but Janey sent her home, saying she wanted to take the night watch. She did not want her cousin to be involved in anything this risky. Emily looked relieved and went off without putting up much of an argument. After losing sleep two nights in a row, the older girl was ready for a good night's rest.

As Janey watched Emily disappear down the street, she felt a pang of guilt at the thought of her mother. Janey knew it wasn't right to make her mother worry, but she couldn't turn back now – not when she was so close to solving the case. No one in the world knew what Janey was planning to do that night. Suddenly, she felt very alone.

She was alone in the passage when the lights in the house went out.

She was alone when the moon rose, casting bright fingers of light over the scene.

She was alone when the Vigilance Committee gang made its noisy way up Pearl Street, cursing and swearing at number 54 as they passed. At least this time they didn't try anything more damaging.

Janey was alone an hour later when she finally slipped out of her hiding spot, ran noiselessly around behind the row of buildings on Pearl Street, and all but flew up the stairs of the neighbouring house. Before she knew it, Janey was standing on a tiny landing, swaying slightly in the winter wind, looking across the small gap between buildings. That was all that stood between her and the ghost house.

The gap wasn't wide – perhaps two feet across, but its height was frightening. Janey wasn't cold, not anymore, but her teeth began to chatter as she looked down at the ground far below. She hesitated. Her plan required her to jump across. One little leap. She'd jumped longer distances before!

But not from so high up, her sensible brain whispered.

Janey felt frozen in place. The wind whipped at her hair and drove needles of ice through her shawl.

"No!" she told herself sternly. "You are not stopping now! What would Holmes do?"

It was the thought of the detective's mocking smile at her ridiculous fear that finally propelled Janey. Taking a deep breath, she braced herself, and then took a flying leap over the gap, landing cat-like on the slanted roof. She'd done it!

Janey took a moment to catch her breath, fear had knocked the wind out of her. But the night's work had only just begun.

The roof slanted down towards the eaves, but the angle was mild. Under normal circumstances, Janey would have had no trouble crawling safely across, but with the rising wind the clouds had returned and a sleety, freezing rain had begun to fall. The roof was getting slipperier by the minute. Janey quickly sat down to avoid losing her balance and sliding right off the roof entirely. She gathered her skirts around her and slowly began to scoot across the roof in a modified crab walk. Carefully and as silently as she could, Janey inched down towards the eave. Finally, she was there! She lay down flat on her stomach, pressing herself into the roof and gripping the edge tightly in her hands. Carefully, she lowered her head over the side. The sleet had wet her hair and the water dripped into her eyes, making it hard to see. Her hands felt frozen to the metal eave, but Janey held fast. She could see no trace of light through the window. Whoever was inside must be sleeping. Good, she thought. That makes things less complicated.

Now came the most dangerous part of her plan. Janey very slowly released her hold on the eaves and reached down to grasp the window frame below her. Very gently – so gently and slowly that it almost didn't move at all – Janey pulled the window open. It seemed to her that it took hours to get it open entirely, but at last it stood open, just below where she lay on the roof.

For the next part, Janey closed her eyes.

She turned her body on the roof, and swung her legs down over the side. Her heart was hammering so hard that blood roared in her ears. Janey thought she might faint. Squeezing her eyes shut tighter, she forced herself to breathe. In and out, in and out went her breath as her feet scrabbled for a hold on the attic windowsill. At last she found it, and inched herself down further until she could, with a twist and a jump, land safely inside the attic. She had done it!

She pulled aside the curtain that had swathed her, thanking her lucky stars that she'd made it in safely. Perhaps all the days of running about on the streets had served her well.

She was surprised to see that the attic wasn't dark after all - a dim flame burned in a storm lantern on the table in the middle of the room.

Looking around, Janey saw that the entire attic was a single, unfinished room. The ceiling was nothing but bare wooden beams, and the angled walls were unpainted and unadorned. The two windows were heavily curtained. Aside from the table, the only other furnishing in the room was a rickety old bed, set into the far corner. It was piled with blankets against the chill that entered through the cracks in the unfinished walls. There was an unlit candle on the floor, and dozens of books and papers heaped untidily around it. A plate with the remnants of that night's dinner sat in the corner, as if pushed aside. Janey moved towards the bed, curious as she always was, about the books. Just as she picked one up, she heard a rustling sound behind her. She whipped around, dropping the book with a dull thud.

Standing not two feet away from her was the ghost. Its face was distorted in a terrible grimace and its skin was a pure, chalky white devoid of all life. There was nothing but cavernous hollows where its eyes should have been. Later Janey would be very proud of herself that she did not scream.

She watched with sick dread as it slowly raised its hand to point an accusing finger at her.

"Who are you?" its shaking voice demanded.

Chapter Twenty-Six

Janey gulped. "Who – who am I?" she repeated stupidly. She felt paralyzed with shock, unable to understand what she was seeing. As if someone else were speaking out of her mouth, she heard herself asking, "Who are *you*?"

"I live here," the ghost replied. Its voice had a scratched, gravelly quality to it that Janey could not quite place. It spoke haltingly, in fits and starts. "And you don't. You should not be here. You must go." Then its voice exploded into a fit of barking coughs. It went on and on, until finally the ghost was leaning over, braced on its own knees as if unable to stand on its own.

Janey's fear gave way to pity. She'd heard similar coughs too often of late to feel anything but pity for the poor creature who was gasping and wheezing before her. Somewhere in the back of her mind, she thought that she'd never heard of a ghost with a cough before.

She rushed over to its side and took its arm – an arm that felt warm in her own, and very much alive. She led the ghost over to the bed and tentatively patted its back while the coughs gradually subsided. Its hands came up and hooked behind its ears, and Janey saw an extraordinary thing. The ghost's entire face came away in its hands. In place of the terrifying, white visage of the ghost was the flushed, serious face of a young boy. Janey recognized it from the locket she'd found.

"A mask!" Janey exclaimed in delight. "I knew it! I

knew you couldn't be a ghost."

The boy was still catching his breath. "I'm not- I'm not a ghost. But-" He paused to take a deep breath. "But it has to be a secret. No one can know I'm here."

"But why?" Janey asked.

The boys' eyes widened suddenly. "Because I'm sick! You have to get away from me or I'll infect you, too! Get away!"

Janey backed up a little, moving away from the bed. The boy looked up at her with sad eyes. "No one is supposed to be near me. Even my mother and father are afraid. They pretend they're not, but I can tell. I'd be afraid too, if I were them."

He was young, Janey saw. Several years younger than she was, and very thin. He looked frail, as if a gust of wind would blow him over.

"What is your name?" she asked.

"It doesn't matter! You have to leave! You can't be here!" His voice was getting stronger now that his coughing fit had passed. Janey was afraid he would wake his parents.

"Hush," she said. "I just want to talk to you. I'll stay over on this side of the room, and you stay on the bed. I'll be quite safe, I promise."

The boy looked doubtful, but nodded.

Janey relaxed, slightly. She sat down on the floor and crossed her legs. She wanted the boy to relax and trust her, so that he would tell her the truth about his situation. There was only one way she knew of gaining somebody's trust, and that was to trust them first.

"My name is Janey. Janey Wiggins," she told him. "Your mask has been frightening people, you know!"

"Has it?" he asked. He seemed to perk up a little at the thought.

"Of course it has. Look at it! It's terrifying. Last week, a man named Mr. Roberts was walking down Pearl Street late at night. He looked up at your house and saw you – it scared the poor man half to death!"

"We didn't– We didn't realize it would be frightening." The boy picked up the mask and turned it over in his hands. "We just needed a way to keep me hidden."

"But why?" Janey asked. She still didn't understand.

"You've already seen," the boy said sadly. "I am sick. I can't stop coughing. We think it's tuberculosis. Mama said that if anyone knew there was a sick child in the house, the doctors would come and take me away from them. I'd be alone in a hospital." He blinked his eyes several times, looking stricken at the thought.

"That's not quite how it works," Janey said gently. Suddenly, the boy seemed very young to her, very innocent in the ways of the world.

"What is your name?" she tried again.

"I am Fritz. I mean, Friedrick Abramowitz." He automatically held out his hand to shake hers. Remembering suddenly that he wasn't supposed to, Fritz pulled it back sharply.

Janey shot him a big, genuine smile. "I'm very pleased to meet you, Fritz."

Fritz just smiled and looked down at his hands. She was beginning to suspect he was rather shy.

"Why are you here?" he whispered.

"I…" Janey was momentarily at a loss. Why *was* she there? This part of the case was properly Holmes's job – he was the detective, the solver of cases. She was nobody. But then she looked over and saw Fritz, saw a sick and scared boy staring at her with a tiny gleam of hope in his eyes. It was a fragile gleam that could be extinguished by fear at any moment. Janey suddenly knew why she was there.

"I'm here to help you," she said firmly. "I am not afraid. I'm here to be your friend."

Fritz looked at Janey quizzically. "I don't understand," he said at last. "Why would you do this for me? Why would you want to be my friend? I am no one, Janey. No one at all."

Janey smiled, thinking of all the things she had learned and experienced in the past few days. "No one is no one, Fritz," she murmured.

She was beginning to believe it.

Chapter Twenty-Seven

Janey and Fritz sat together in that cold attic, talking and talking, getting to know each other. Janey learned that Fritz's family had only recently moved to London. They had come from Russia in search of work for Fritz's father, and safety for the family. They were Jewish; Russia had become a dangerous place for them.

"So I was right!" Janey exclaimed. Fritz went on with his story.

It was on the long journey to London that Fritz had fallen ill with his cough. When they realized how serious the tuberculosis outbreak was in their new neighbourhood, Fritz's parents had been terrified. They heard from their new neighbours about the locked hospitals for infectious diseases where sick patients were isolated from the world. The family grew terrified that their son would be taken away from them, lost forever, if anyone were to find out that he was ill.

"I couldn't be separated from them," Fritz explained tearfully to Janey. "I need my mama and papa. If I were taken from them... Well, I would not recover."

Janey felt tears prick at her own eyes. "I understand why you were afraid," she said. "I promise you, that will never happen."

Hours passed as they talked, but to the children, it felt like only minutes. Janey told Fritz all about life with her mother, about leaving school and working with the flower women at Covent Garden, and how desperately she yearned for an education. She realized, halfway through, that she'd never told anyone about this before. It felt like a weight lifted off her shoulders.

Fritz told Janey about his life in Russia, about the school he had attended, about the friends he had grown up with, and about how much he missed them. He, too, longed to return to school – for he had not attended a single class since they had left Russia.

"My parents speak no English although I am trying to teach them," he said at last.

"And how did you learn?"

"From books," Fritz said with a shrug. "My papa gave me a dictionary that shows English words beside Russian words, and lots of other books to practice on. It has kept me occupied while I've been sick. Mama says it's good for me to stay busy, it keeps me from being sad."

"Is that why you have so many books in your house?" Janey asked suddenly.

Fritz looked at her strangely. "How do you know how many books we have?"

Janey blushed, then. "Do you remember the thumping on the attic door earlier today?"

Fritz nodded.

"That was me. I was looking for you."

Fritz's eyes widened. "You scared me half to death!"

he exclaimed. "I thought that the terrible men were back to hurt papa – or that the doctors had come to take me away!"

Janey shook her head. "I'm so sorry I frightened you. But no. That's not how doctors do things here. I don't think your parents quite understood. No one will come and drag you away by force. I promise! If you have tuberculosis, there are hospitals you can go to. You can stay there until you're well again – and they will want to keep you, to prevent you from infecting anyone else. It is only to help you, to care for you. But, Fritz, I don't believe you need to worry about that."

Janey made a very brave decision, then. She stood and walked over to where Fritz sat shivering on the bed. She picked up a blanket and wrapped it carefully around his shoulders, then sat down next to him. She had to make him believe she was not afraid of his illness.

"Oh!" Janey realized suddenly. "I know a doctor! He would take good care of you, Fritz. He'd fix you up in no time. His name is Doctor Watson, and he's the kindest man you ever met in your life!"

"Not kinder than my papa is," Fritz said loyally.

"Well, perhaps not," Janey said, smiling. "But he has been very kind to me. I'm sure he can help you."

Janey was about to tell Fritz all about Mr. Holmes and Dr. Watson when there was a tremendous crash. The house itself seemed to shake in its foundations, as if something heavy were battering it from the outside. Janey and Fritz looked at each other with frightened eyes.

There came another crash, then a woman's scream, and the sound of men shouting.

"Mama! Papa!" Fritz cried. Throwing off the blanket, he flew to the attic door and had it unbarred in an instant. Before Janey could move, he disappeared down the stairs into the darkness and chaos of the house below.

Chapter Twenty-Eight

When Janey emerged from the attic, the house below was to a scene of great confusion and uproar. Mrs. Abramowitz stood in a corner in her nightdress, holding up a candle that provided only dim illumination of the room. Her husband was in front of her, facing two men who had just battered his front door down.

Everyone was shouting. No one could hear a thing. Holmes's voice was in full thunder, demanding that the man and woman produce the child they had stolen away and hidden in their attic. His eyes were flinty and cold. Watson echoed Holmes, asking again and again where the child was, as his eyes darted around the house as if searching for hidey holes. In the corner, Mr. Abramowitz was shouting back in Russian, clearly demanding that these strangers leave his home. His wife behind him shrank back in fear.

Janey saw Fritz standing, petrified, at the bottom of the stairs. He was trembling with fear, his face was wet with tears as he stared with horror at the confrontation – and Janey's skin prickled hot with rage.

"*Stop this at once!*" she cried, stomping her foot for good measure.

The surprise of a young girl's voice raised in anger in the middle of such chaos was enough to shock everyone into silence. Holmes and Watson glanced at each other in consternation when they saw Janey. Mr. and Mrs. Abramowitz gaped openly.

Janey walked down the rest of the stairs to take Fritz's trembling hand. "Don't be afraid," she whispered. "I know these men. I will put this right." She led Fritz over to the group of adults by his hand. "Mr. Holmes," she said, "I'd like to introduce you to the Pearl Street ghost. This is Fritz Abramowitz – he is Mr. and Mrs. Abramowitz's son."

Holmes's eyes widened. He looked between the boy and his parents, his mouth gaping in surprise. Then he knelt down and gripped Fritz gently by the shoulders. "Is this true?" he asked at last, looking piercingly into the boy's eyes. "You are their son?"

Fritz nodded.

Janey turned to him. "Go to your parents," she told him. "Tell them they have nothing to fear, that we will explain everything. These men are not members of the Vigilance Committee gang, and they're not here to take you away – at least they won't be, once I get through with them," she finished, shooting daggers at her employers.

Fritz ran to his mother. His parents gathered him up in their arms, pulling him into a corner as far from Holmes and Watson as they could. Meanwhile, Janey tugged the men angrily to the door.

"You have frightened this good family half to death!" Janey exclaimed furiously. "It was not at all necessary. It is just as I told you, and if you had believed me in the first place, this," she gestured to the family in the corner, tearful and afraid, "would never have happened. They are a kind family. There has been no kidnapping."

Holmes sat back on his heels with a stunned expression on his face. "It makes no sense," he murmured. "All the clues pointed to kidnapping. What have I missed?"

He looked so shocked by his own failure, his usual confidence so completely shaken, that Janey almost forgot her anger. She began to feel a little sorry for him.

"Sometimes, Mr. Holmes, people are good and kind. You mustn't forget that."

He looked at her with startled eyes, and nodded. "There is a surprising streak of wisdom in you," he said slowly. "Thank you. It's a good reminder to carry with me."

Beside him, Watson smiled his kindly smile at Janey. She felt warm with their approval.

"And now, we need to put this right," Holmes said, walking slowly to the family huddled in the corner.

By now, Fritz had given his parents some explanation as to who Janey was and reassured them of their safety. They were calmed and, to Janey's relief, they looked more curious rather than upset.

Holmes approached them, kneeling down before Fritz. "It appears that I have made a dreadful mistake. It does not happen often, but when it does, I own up to it. Please tell your parents I am sorry for frightening them. It was an error. I feared for your safety, and I was wrong."

He paused, while Fritz translated this for Mr. and Mrs. Abramowitz.

The couple nodded in understanding. They whispered

137

to each other, and then spoke to Fritz. Holmes looked at him, questioningly.

"They asked me to thank you for your concern for me, Mr. Holmes. They want you to know that I am loved and cared for. There is no need for anyone to worry about me."

Holmes smiled, and held out his hand. Mr. Abramowitz shook it, tentatively at first, but then more heartily, and then Mrs. Abramowitz shook it as well.

Everything seemed to be turning out perfectly, Janey thought happily.

Then Fritz began to cough.

Chapter Twenty-Nine

In the blink of an eye, Fritz's mother scooped up the coughing boy and ran with him up the stairs to the attic, slamming the door behind her. Holmes and Watson looked on in confusion.

"They think he has tuberculosis," she explained to them. "They fear the doctors will take him away if he's discovered."

Holmes raised his eyebrows, but Dr. Watson was shaking his head. "That did not sound like a tubercular cough to me," he said. "If anything, it had the sound of chronic, untreated bronchitis. Sir," he added, turning to Fritz's father, "I am a doctor. I would like to examine your son. I promise you that I will not take him away without your permission, regardless of his illness."

Mr. Abramowitz shook his head. He did not understand English. But then suddenly, his eyes blazed with fear. "Doctor?" he asked, in a trembling, heavily-accented voice. Janey could see the terror in his eyes.

"Yes!" Watson replied. "Doctor! But I will not take him. I can help."

Mr. Abramowitz took a deep breath. Janey saw the fear in his eyes warring with concern for his son. Finally, he nodded his head as if he understood. Perhaps he knew more English than he had let on. He led Dr. Watson up the stairs to the attic, calling for his wife. When the door swung open, the two men disappeared into the room.

Janey and Holmes were left alone. Without a word, they moved toward the fireplace where the coals of the banked fire still gave off a little heat amid the chilled air. They made themselves comfortable in the armchairs.

Holmes looked at her narrowly as Janey held her hands out to pick up the heat. "This case has been an excellent example to you, and I hope that your education will profit from my error. Do you recall? I once told you that one of the most important rules of detection is that the simplest explanation is usually the correct one – no matter how much we want the fantastic to be true. Tonight you have seen the disastrous result from ignoring this rule. I wanted to see a crime in Fritz's confinement, so I did. The simpler explanation did not occur to me."

Janey plucked up her courage and spoke her mind. "Something of the sort did occur to *me*, sir, but my opinion meant nothing to you."

Holmes bowed his head. "You're right. That was my second error - I underestimated you. I am sorry, Miss Wiggins." He thought for a moment, then spoke again, "I have a favour to ask. If, in our future cases together, you notice that I am getting arrogant and over-confident, that I am not listening to the truth when it is spoken, I would be very grateful if you would whisper the words 'Pearl Street Ghost' in my ear."

Janey couldn't help it, then – she giggled out loud. She doubted she would ever have the nerve to say such a thing to Mr. Holmes, but was relieved to hear that there would be future cases. Holmes still wanted her, even though she had proven him wrong!

They heard footsteps, then, and the attic door opened. Down came Dr. Watson, behind him followed Fritz and his parents.

"Let him be warm by the fire," Dr. Watson was saying. "Let him rest happy, let him see friends – Janey, if she likes – and he'll soon be right as rain. Why, you can even send him to school! I shall send along some vitamins that will make him stronger than ever."

With shining eyes, Fritz translated his words to his parents, who smiled widely.

"It's as I suspected," Watson explained to Holmes and Janey. "His cough is not tubercular. There is no blood in his sputum, no fever, and his parents remain uninfected. He has a nasty case of chronic bronchitis, brought on by the hardships of his journey to England. He will recover entirely, given enough time and rest."

Mr. Abramowitz had tears in his eyes as he shook Dr. Watson's hand, thanking him in broken English. Mrs. Abramowitz clasped Fritz in her arms.

Janey sat back in her chair, pleased as punch that Fritz would soon be healthy again. Healthy and in school. That stung a little, if she were to be honest with herself - that he would have a chance to go where she so desperately wished to. But she had a different future in store for her; one full adventure and mystery with her wonderful new friends. So many adventures! She was, after all, a Baker Street Irregular. The fire blurred before her eyes as Janey's head grew heavy with sleep. It was so very late. Perhaps she might close her eyes, just a little...

"Come, Janey," Holmes said, shaking her gently by the shoulder. It might have been minutes or hours later. "Let's get you home."

Janey let out an enormous yawn and stood. She didn't even want to think about how she would explain being out all night to her mother, who was no doubt frantic with worry.

Fritz smiled shyly at her. "I hope to see you again," he said.

She took his hand and promised to come visit him soon.

Dr. Watson took up her shawl and wrapped it tightly around Janey. He pressed a crown coin into her hand with a smile. "I'd say you've more than earned your pay, Miss Wiggins," he said, and she glowed with pride.

She couldn't wait to tell Emily and Rose all about it, and give her pay to her mother!

Mr. and Mrs. Abramowitz saw them to the door as the detectives took their leave. Together, the three of them turned and walked out into the pink dawn of the rising sun.

Also from Orange Pip Books

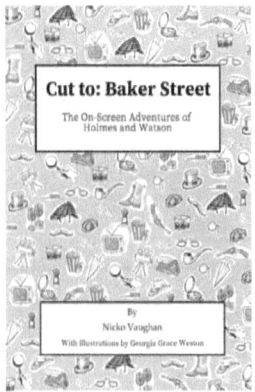

It is well documented that Sherlock Holmes is the most depicted literary character on screen; he even has an entry in the Guinness Book of Records to prove it. This reference guide covers depictions of the world's most famous detective, and his faithful companion, from the first silent film Sherlock Holmes is Baffled (1900) to the Will Ferrell, John C. Reilly comedy Holmes and Watson (2018). As well as cinema and television portrayals, this book by Nicko Vaughan (Author of The Wordy Companion: An A-Z Guide to Sherlockian Phraseology) also covers documentaries, animations and web series adaptations alongside début feature artwork by graphic artist Georgia Grace Weston.

Combining encyclopaedia, biography and reference structure, this book comprehensively explores the many celluloid faces, cathode-ray shapes and digital sizes of Sherlock Holmes and Doctor John Watson, so far.

Violet Holmes is not an ordinary teenager because, well, nothing is ordinary when you're the adopted daughter of the great Sherlock Holmes. Having been home schooled for her entire life she has decided to take the plunge, at 14, and attend Bardle Secondary School to study for her exams. But after a week, she notices that the school hides a deep secret, and she's determined to crack it wide open. Are the current spate of school thefts the work of criminal masterminds? Is there really a secret society behind closed doors? Can a girl like Violet make friends and fit in?

Also from Orange Pip Books

Just the place for a Nark!" the Detective cried,
As he eagerly surveyed the scene;
With the stout-hearted Doctor alert at his side,
And the Dog standing guard in between.

Imagine a world where the logic of Sherlock Holmes meets the nonsense of Wonderland! *The Hunting of the Nark* combines the best of Lewis Carroll and Arthur Conan Doyle's adventures into a madcap collection of verse, including the novella-length case, *The Adventure of the Twinkling Hat*. Holmes and Watson will discover that anything can happen at 221B when you're the White Knight...

Dr. John H. Watson is a man of medical science, a man of action and a man of letters. His life has been one of adventure and romance. In 1894 he finds himself alone following the death of his great friend Sherlock Holmes three years earlier and now the passing of his beloved wife, Mary. His loneliness is all encompassing and only a true friend can help him to see there is still reason to continue living. But when that friend, Inspector G. Lestrade of Scotland Yard suddenly and mysteriously disappears, Dr. Watson takes it upon himself to discover the reason for the abduction.

It wasn't that John couldn't tell the story. It wasn't that we didn't know the truth. It was that nobody would believe us. But we cannot keep Sherlock alive with silence. The reader smiles when Moriarty appears on the page. So does Moriarty. And Sherlock Holmes follows him. We smile because we recognise them. Scarlett Vendalle is recognised by nobody, except for John Watson. With no recollection of her own identity and a suspected criminal past, Scarlett is the perfect case for Sherlock. As they follow her tracks, red threads appear in their lives that make it more than clear - Scarlett meeting John and Sherlock was no coincidence. Someone has drawn her shadow on the wall before she appeared. Was it Anne Boleyn who haunts Scarlett with visions of her past? Was it Moriarty who attracts Sherlock like a magnet? Or was it another shadow from the past? With Moriarty's men on the one hand and the secret service on the other, the stage is set for a game with deadly rules, as Sherlock, John and Scarlett slowly become aware that something larger is guiding their steps...
Is there another story being written…?

Also from Orange Pip Books

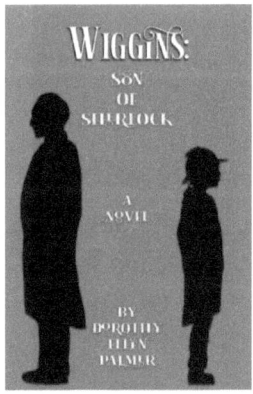

On New Year's Day 1891, Sherlock Holmes summons the limping street urchin, Wiggins, to Baker Street and decrees he must die at dawn. Wiggins, however, has other plans. To fulfil the dying wish of his mother, Irene Adler, he schemes with his two formidable American aunties to keep two important facts from the great detective: Mrs. Hudson is actually his Aunt Grizelda, and he is both Holmes' child and a girl pretending to be a boy. Through a series of mysterious letters Adler bequeathed to Wiggins, the dark backstory of her parents and all their long-kept family secrets unravel. To flee the mad King of Bohemia trying to claim Wiggins as his heir, Holmes and Wiggins begin their Great Hiatus. From Mycroft to Moriarty, from Dr. John H. Watson to the Baker Street Irregulars, from P.T. Barnum to Jumbo the Elephant, Wiggins learns little is what it seems. Slowly learning to trust each other, Holmes and Wiggins travel from London to Reichenbach Falls to New York City to a small farm in Canada which holds the secrets of their family history. Together, they correct the errors in Watson's tales, bond over Wiggins' disability, drop their masquerades, and deduce a father and daughter future.